BOOKS BY JOAB STIEGLITZ

The Utgarda Trilogy

The Old Man's Request

The Missing Medium

The Other Realm

The Thule Trilogy

The Hunter in the Shadows:

The Hunter in the Shadows

Book Four of the Utgarda Series

Joab Stieglitz

Copyright © 2019 Joab Stieglitz
All rights reserved.
Cover illustration by Eugene Chugunov
ISBN: 9781099881091

This is a work of fiction. Names, characters, businesses, places, events and incidents are either the products of the author's imagination or used in a fictitious manner. Any resemblance to actual persons, living or dead, or actual events is purely coincidental.

Published in the United States by Rantings of a Wandering Mind

The Hunter in the Shadows

Joab Stieglitz

DEDICATION

This book is dedicated to my wife, without whose continual support and relentless encouragement it may never have been finished.

Joab Stieglitz

ACKNOWLEDGMENTS

I would like to acknowledge all the people who inspired, encouraged, assisted, and supported me through this effort.

Many thanks to Steph, Greg, Jenna, and Josiah for wading through my drafts and proposing, or demanding, edits, changes, and other suggestions.

Thanks to the Springfield Writers group for listening, critiquing, and suggesting things that made the story all the better, especially Carol, David, Fred, and Duane.

Joab Stieglitz

The Hunter in the Shadows

Chapter 1

March 9, 1930

The air was thick and heavy, permeated with the smell of decomposing vegetation. Anna Rykov stepped carefully through the lush foliage. She had a machete in one hand and her revolver in the other. Sweat poured into her eyes from beneath her pith helmet, and her khaki shirt and trousers were already soaked through. The canteen on her belt was nearly empty.

The German was just ahead. The drops of blood were getting closer together, indicating that the wounded man was starting to slow down. Eventually, she would find von Juntz, and he would get his comeuppance.

Anna stepped carefully. Wolfram von Juntz had been at the site for some time. Who knew what manner of traps and tripwires he had lain. Still, he did not appear to be taking special care. His path through the undergrowth was evident, and it was more or less straight. Between the uneven footing among the thick vines that criss-crossed the ground, the wide-leaved bushes, the tall palms that blocked the sunlight, and the ever-present mist that limited visibility even further, Anna had to be careful.

The Hunter in the Shadows

Anna climbed over a tree trunk that had fallen across the trail she and her quarry had been following and was startled by a leering face in the foliage. She immediately realized it was a statue. She stopped and listened, attempting to ascertain von Juntz's location, but she heard nothing. The cries of the monkeys and birds were gone.

Anna approached the clearing cautiously. She stopped short of the tree line to take in a Mesoamerican-style complex. The buildings were set in the middle of a stagnant lake. Greenish algae coated its surface, obscuring whatever lurked below. Here and there, Anna saw bubbles, indicating some kind of movement under the water.

The staring face was in the form of a dragon-like head, and it was one of a pair mounted on each side of an ornamental wall on either side of the entrance to the city. From the colorful and fairly fresh iconography, Anna could tell that the site was not Mayan in origin, nor that of any other Central American civilization she was aware of.

There were a dozen or so adobe-style structures. Each sat on an artificial platform connected to others by narrow walkways. In the center of the complex was a wide-open area, beyond which was a stepped pyramid. Something seemed strange about the pyramid, and it took a moment for Anna to realize that it had only three sides, rather than the usual four, with two of the sides visible to her.

Anna crouched behind a bush and observed the scene, looking for signs of movement or anything else that might betray von Juntz's location. Large insects pestered her, and it took all of her resolve to ignore them. Just when she was about to give up, Anna heard two gunshots from within the ancient complex. She scanned the landscape, and this time she saw the blond archaeologist limping from a building on the right toward the central square.

Anna leapt out of the foliage and ran between the dragon statues. As soon as she stepped onto the path, the walkway dipped under her weight. The path was not stationary — it was floating on the surface. Two more gunshots rang out inside the building von Juntz had emerged from.

Anna fought to regain her balance. Once stable, she looked closely at the footing and saw that the walkway was made from wide bamboo stalks lashed together. She scanned the area, but there was no sign of von Juntz. Then Anna noticed several trails of bubbles rising from the muck and moving toward her.

Using the balance and reflexes she had acquired in the land of Brian Teplow's visions, Anna expertly crossed the gap to the square and stepped onto the solid stone foundation as several gavials, large, narrow-jawed crocodiles, snapped at the bamboo. The wood was too unstable for the giant creatures to climb onto the path, and the platform had concave sides clearly designed to prevent them from doing so.

Anna took a moment to catch her breath. The thick, fetid air was nauseating, and she tried not to breathe through her nose. After a moment, she led with the revolver and advanced toward the pyramid.

◆

Anna crossed the square carefully. She noted the mosaic pattern laid into the surface resembled the dragon head on the gate posts. On closer inspection, she realized that it was not a dragon head, but rather that of a crocodile. The image was anthropomorphic and wearing a golden headdress that draped over and past its shoulders. The body was male, dressed in a white loincloth over its scaly, green skin. It had golden cuffs beset with green gems. Its hands were splayed, revealing long, imposing claws.

Anna's inspection was interrupted by a cry of pain from a structure to her right, the one that von Juntz had emerged from. Anna approached the structure cautiously, testing the walkway to that platform before moving onto it. It was also floating on the surface, and Anna stepped quickly but lightly, crossing the gap before the creatures below could react.

The path ended at the darkened opening to the structure, but there was a dim light coming from a space beyond the initial room. Anna waited a moment for her eyes to adjust to the darkness before entering. As she did so, luminescent qualities in the artwork on the walls made the imagery seem to leap out in three dimensions all around her.

Insubstantial humanoid and non-humanoid creatures were gathered in worship and ceremony, including insect-men similar to those serving Queen Sif of Brynner; the Pointee goat-man followers of Goh-Bazh; and the large-eyed, large-eared Draunskur of the Endless Barrens. As Anna moved about the scene, the imagery moved along with her. There were no sounds or smells, but the visuals made it seem as if she was among the crowd gathered on the central platform.

As she looked about at the scene projected all around her in the chamber, a procession of beings emerged from the jungle, passed between the gates, and crossed the walkway just as she had. Crocodile-men armed with spears appeared first, escorting a prisoner bound with ropes. The blond-haired woman walked solemnly, her head bowed. She wore a wide, green, beaded collar around her neck that revealed the bottom of her breasts, and a matching beaded loincloth. Both the collar and the loincloth were embroidered with the image depicted in the mosaic in the plaza.

As the visionary procession passed by, the crowd hissed and made rude gestures at the captive. When one cat-headed being attempted to hit the prisoner, a soldier speared the would-be attacker and threw her behind him over his head. The cat-lady flew free of the spear and landed somewhere in the lake out of Anna's view, but Anna was distracted when the prisoner looked up and made eye contact with her. It was Sobak, her little sister from the world of Brian Teplow's visions. The girl looked to be slightly older than when Anna had last seen her — perhaps sixteen. Her eyes were lined by dark rings of black paint that ran with her tears down her cheeks. She silently mouthed, *Nygof, help me,* with a pleading look.

Suddenly, an enormous crocodile man, the original from which the statues and iconography were made, towered into view, his bare chest visible over the crowd that swarmed around him. When Anna turned back, Sobak had moved on, now at the foot of the steps to the pyramid.

Anna's gaze returned to the giant being, who acknowledged the admiring crowd, glancing to each side in turn. His shadow passed over Anna as he looked in her direction. They made eye contact, and Anna thought his gaze lingered for a moment. Then the giant crocodile followed Sobak and her escorts up the steps of the pyramid. Once at the top, the object of the assembly's admiration stood behind Sobak with his long-clawed hands resting on her shoulders. Then the spectacle faded, and Anna steadied herself against the wall of the darkened chamber.

When the room stopped spinning, Anna considered what she had just seen. Surely the vision was of some time in the ancient past. Yet her fictional sister, from the imagination of retired spiritualist Brian Teplow, had been in the scene and had recognized Anna as her alter-ego, Nygof. Anna tried to replay the vision, but nothing she tried was successful.

Anna followed the light into a smaller chamber. There she found a portly, older man dressed in explorer's khakis lying face down in the corner. Anna could see the dark stains of gunshot wounds in the back of his shirt. The light came from a lantern, which sat on the floor on the other side of the body.

Anna knelt next to the man and felt his neck for a pulse. He was alive. She raised the lantern and set it on a pedestal, where it illuminated the whole room. Anna estimated that the man was in his fifties or sixties. He had thinning white hair and mutton chops. Anna rolled the man over onto his back. She noticed that the bullets had entered from the front, but the smallish wounds and trivial amount of blood on his back were inconsistent with chest wounds. And there was little blood staining the floor where he had lain.

Anna had started unbuttoning the shirt to examine the wounds more closely, when the man's hand reached up and gently grabbed her wrist.

"Excuse me, my dear" his aging, English-accented voice said, "but we haven't been properly introduced."

Chapter 2

March 9, 1930

"How are you not dead?" Anna asked the old man as he rose to a sitting position against the wall.

"Oh," the man said with false modesty, "just lucky I guess."

"Who are you?" Anna said with suspicion, "And what are you doing here?"

"I could ask the same of you, young lady," the man said with a schoolmaster's tone. Then he softened. "My name is Dr. Cornelius Lyton, and I am an archaeologist, currently with the Royal Academy. I was looking for the key to enter the main temple there. I thought I had found it, but then that von Juntz chappie appeared, shot me, and ran off with it." He glanced at Anna. "Well, that's my bit. Now, what's a pretty, young, Russian woman such as yourself doing in a place like this?"

Anna thought for a moment. Prior to running through the jungle after von Juntz, she had no idea where she had come from or why she was there. All she knew was that she had to stop von Juntz. Stop him from what? She did not know.

"I am pursuing Wolfram von Juntz," she said with reservations. "I must catch him before he does something terrible."

"Really? What?!"

"I do not know."

Lyton did not appear to be satisfied with her response, but seemed to let it pass.

"Well, you have your reasons, and now I have mine. I suggest we pool our resources and give that scoundrel his due!"

"What do you have to offer me?" Anna asked.

"I know this site fairly well," Lyton replied with confidence. "Aside from the pyramid, I have explored all the structures on this side of the central plaza. Von Juntz and I ran into each other early on, and we agreed that I would stay west of the plaza, and he would stay to the east. I kept my end of the bargain, but von Juntz had been spying on me over the past few weeks."

"How do you know?"

"I found my notebooks open to different pages, various artifacts had been moved from where I had left them, and so forth. I don't know why he was so keen to see my findings, but for whatever reason, I seem to have found what he was looking for."

"Do you know where he went?"

"I expect that he went to the chamber at the top of the pyramid. There is an indentation with a distorted human face set into the floor there. It is the only iconography on the entire pyramid structure. The figurine that sat on that pedestal appeared to fit precisely into the mouth of that face."

"Do you know what is inside the pyramid?"

"That would be telling," Lyton said, "as if you don't know." He stood, seeming no worse for having been shot, and dusted off his clothing. "We best get after him," the Englishman said, indicating the door to Anna.

Anna and Lyton both expertly crossed the floating walkway and the central plaza to the pyramid. About halfway up the steps, Anna stopped to help the old man.

"I usually take a short break every ten steps or so," he said apologetically.

"It would be better to reach the top alive than not at all," Anna replied, "You are of no help to me if you have a heart attack."

Lyton eyed Anna appraisingly.

"Spoken like a Russian," he said coldly. Anna ignored the comment.

"Von Juntz is already there," Anna said. "He can wait for us until we are ready. Unless we need to stop him from completing whatever he has in mind."

Lyton shook his head.

"For all I know, he expects to find riches that he wants to keep for himself," Lyton said flatly. "I expect he will be disappointed. If he has any other motivation, I am not aware of it." They waited a moment in silence until Lyton had caught his breath, then continued. They stopped two more times before they reached the top.

The triangular platform on top of the pyramid was roughly five feet on a side. Within a foot-wide lip on the surface there had once been some kind of door, but now the space was empty, revealing a dark shaft below. A thick rope had been tied to a stake that had been hammered into the stone, its end disappearing into the darkness. A reptilian gargoyle was mounted in the center of each of the three sides of the shaft peered up malevolently at the two about ten feet below the opening.

Anna looked to Lyton, but it was clear that the old man would be unable to climb down the rope.

"How did you intend to explore this structure?" she asked.

"I hadn't expected a pyramid such as this to be hollow," Lyton said sheepishly. "I presumed that there would be a side entrance to an altar at the top, as with other Mesoamerican pyramids."

"Well, my arrival appears to be fortuitous for you," Anna said. "I will climb down the rope and see what is to be found. You wait here." Lyton nodded. Anna glanced at the thick, rough rope, and then said. "Give me your handkerchief." Lyton did so without hesitation, and Anna tied it around her left hand. As she did so, Lyton produced another from his pocket. When Anna was finished, he tied it around her right hand. "Thank you."

Anna sat with her legs over the lip of the opening. She wrapped her legs around the rope, and then slowly slid over the edge, taking hold of it before dropping her shoulders through the gap. She crawled carefully down the rope into the abyss. As her eyes adjusted to the darkness, Anna noticed that the walls of the shaft were wet, and as she descended the humidity within the pyramid grew as well, and a gibbering sound floated up from below.

Anna continued her descent. The air had become so thick, and the smell of rotting vegetation so strong, that she fought to breathe in the foul atmosphere.

"How is it going?" Lyton shouted from above, startling Anna, who lost her grip and slid a short distance. She could feel raw abrasions on her thighs, and a burning sensation as they were irritated by the sweat streaming off her.

"I am well," Anna said through gritted teeth. "Please allow me to concentrate." She looked down and spotted a ledge a few feet lower. "I think I am nearing the bottom."

Anna noticed the dim light from above fade, and then there was a crack and a cry as the old Englishman fell past Anna to land a short distance below her with a soft thud. The gibbering sound resumed and seemed even closer.

"Are you all right?" Anna said anxiously. She heard groaning and could barely make out his form sprawled below her. Anna was within jumping distance of the floor, though the triangular shaft continued through it into unknown depths.

She slid onto the floor and knelt beside Lyton. The elderly man had managed to fall onto the remains of a large bush. On closer inspection, he had landed on something on top of the bush. It was a man. Wolfram von Juntz lay sprawled beneath Lyton. There was a bullet hole smack in the center of the German's forehead.

Anna glanced from side to side, looking for the shooter. From what she could see, the rope was the only way out, aside from the hole in the floor. The chamber was littered with plants and small animals, all in a state of decay. Lyton stirred.

"Are you hurt?" Anna asked. Lyton sat up slowly and looked around.

"Only my pride," he said with a wry smile. "Von Juntz here seems to have broken my fall!"

"He was shot," Anna said, "and the shooter must still be here somewhere." Lyton glanced around the chamber.

"Where?" the Englishman said with skepticism. "There are no other chambers here, and the only way out is…" He glanced up at the rope. "Oh, dear."

"There is also that opening in the floor," Anna said, directing his gaze to it. "Perhaps there is an exit below."

Satisfied, Lyton started searching von Juntz's pockets. When he removed a small notebook from a shirt pocket, he quickly flipped through the pages, on which Anna could see handwritten notes scribbled in German. As he flipped through the pages, one fell out. Anna quickly stooped over and picked it up, but Lyton was too focused on the notebook and had not noticed. Glancing at the paper, she saw a carefully drawn depiction of the design in the plaza — the same design that was on Sobak's clothing. She folded the page and put it in her own pocket.

Still wary of potential attackers, Anna glanced around the room as she crawled to the lip of the hole. She peered down as Lyton appeared at her side, and noted what looked like a ladder set into one side with unusual characters carved into the wall between the rungs.

"Those glyphs are common througohut the complex," Lyton said, "but I hadn't begun translating them yet." Anna recognized the writing. It was similar to that which Brian Teplow had translated while under hypnosis. "Von Juntz has noted various glyphs in his notebook, but had only translated a handful of characters." He flipped through the book, looking for the glyphs in view. "It seems as if the language is ideographic. Von Juntz has noted several possible meanings next to several of them." He continued flipping. "But none of these have been translated."

"It seems to continue down the ladder," Anna noted. "Perhaps it is meant to be said while descending."

"Some kind of prayer or incantation, you think?" Lyton asked. Anna nodded.

"But we do not know how to read or pronounce them," she said evenly. "We must proceed anyway." Anna looked down into the opening and tried to make out what was below, but the abyss seemed bottomless. The rotting smell was replaced by a gust of comparatively fresh, warm humidity.

"Maybe there are side passages from this shaft that we just can't see from here," Lyton suggested with a hopeful expression.

"Perhaps," Anna said, then climbed feet first down the ladder cut into the wall. As soon as her hands took hold of the rungs, she realized how sweaty she was. Her fingers barely gripped the smooth stone which was worn in the center. She quickly found some remaining texture along the sides of the rungs. "Keep your feet in the center of the steps and grab toward the sides of the rungs with your hands."

Slowly and carefully, Anna descended. Her feet slipped on almost every step, but she gradually climbed down the rungs. Anna could hear Lyton muttering obscenities, and dirt and debris rained on her from his misplaced steps. She climbed much faster than he did, even at a careful pace, so the Englishman was barely visible in the darkness, perhaps twenty feet above her.

They climbed for an unknown length of time. With all of Lyton's complaining, it seemed like an eternity to Anna, but was probably only a few minutes.

Each step was becoming more difficult. The muscles in Anna's arms and legs were aching, but there was no indication of a bottom or even a landing below her. The debris that passed by Anna fell without ever striking anything below. Perhaps the shaft was bottomless. Yet the sides had clearly been engineered. Aside from the ladder and the glyphs between the rungs, the walls were made of smooth stone fit so tightly together that the seams were barely visible.

Then it dawned on Anna that the exits were probably concealed in the stonework. She stopped her descent and looked closely at the walls surrounding her. Her eyes had adjusted to the near-total darkness, and she could make out the lines of the seams. All she had to do was find evidence of and air passage. It was a long shot. The chambers beyond may not open up to the surface, or not anymore. The secret doors had probably not been opened in centuries, so the gaps could possibly be packed with ancient sediment. But she had to try.

Anna held tightly onto the stones and blew into the visible seams. As expected, dust cleared from the spaces, but unexpectedly swirled around her, getting into her eyes, mouth, and nose. Uncontrollably, Anna sneezed, the lurch of it carrying her away from the wall. Her hands lost their grip, and she tumbled, falling face first.

Anna was frozen in terror. She seemed to fall for an eternity. Absolute blackness stretched all around. She was moving too fast for her eyes to focus on anything. A whooshing sound flooded her ears, but that faint, gibbering sound persisted, and was still audible above it all. Then, there was nothing.

Chapter 3

March 9, 1930

Anna awakened with a start. She was in darkness, surrounded by warm, soft, furry wrappings. There was light interspersed among the coverings, and at her movement, a thumping motion shook the area. She kicked with her arms and legs, the warm fur leapt away, and sunlight flooded the chamber.

Cletus, the large, black, barrel-chested mutt with a white stripe down his eyes and around his muzzle, wagged his tail, which thumped loudly against the floor, his tongue lolling in a doggy grin. Anna had adopted the dog when the Junazhi, inter-dimensional insectoid aliens, had failed to reassemble his owner's frozen and shattered body.

Anna was in her bed. With the blankets and Cletus now on the floor, she was overcome by the chill. Bright sunlight shone through the window, reflected off the snow-covered landscape outside. It was cold for March in Wellersburg, and the late snowfall had left a foot of accumulation on the ground, accompanied by a blustery, chilling wind. She shuddered involuntarily as a gust rattled the panes of her bedroom window.

Anna glanced at the alarm clock on the nightstand. She had not bothered to set the alarm. She had nowhere to go.

While the small university town and surrounding farms had been largely spared from the aftermath of the stock market crash and the drought that had struck the Midwest, the town had been flooded with people from the city looking for work. As a result, indigent care had become a priority of Reister University. Her one colleague, Dr. Harold Lamb, was spending long hours at the hospital tending to the less fortunate, while Father Sean O'Malley was busy ministering to the downtrodden at Saint Michael's Church.

Anna had not been so overcome by events. Attendance at the university had dropped, and the need for adjunct professors along with it. Since Fyodor Rykov, Anna's late husband, had been paranoid enough to commit his fortune to precious metals and stones, Anna's own finances had actually increased in value with the decline in paper investments. Insulated from the harsh realities around her, and without any pressing responsibilities, Anna had fallen into a torpor.

The potential of the Longborough Foundation for Ethnographic Research had yet to be realized. Anna had started documenting the events of the Longborough Affair, as it was now being called, in more detail, but in the absence of Lamb and O'Malley's contributions, or any sense of urgency, her enthusiasm had waned. Anna had not left her house, aside from taking Cletus for walks, since the coming of the late winter chill, with most of that time spent under the warm covers of her bed.

"It is good to see you again, too," she said, reaching out to pat the mutt's head.

Anna climbed lazily out of bed, stretching as she rose, and donned her slippers. She pulled a thick cotton bathrobe from her closet. When she put it on over her pajamas, the stiffness of her shirt pocket caught her attention. Anna removed a faded slip of paper from the pocket. It was the folded sheet from von Juntz's notebook in her dream.

"How did that get there?" she said to Cletus. The dog cocked his head with curiosity.

Now thoroughly awake, Anna stepped from the bedroom, and crossed the hallway to the room she used as an office. The bulk of the two-story house that she rented was empty. The majority of the missing owner's belongings were stored in the basement. Anna knew what had happened to Meyer Kovacs, the Reister University anthropologist who owned the house and had become a powerful sorcerer in the imaginary world created by the mystic, Brian Teplow, but his demise was not generally known. The unnerving gaze from the portrait of Kovac's late wife seemed to follow Anna as she crossed the length of the hall.

The office was even colder than the rest of the house. Anna had not been in there in over a week, and she kept the doors closed to contain Cletus' wanderings. The room was sparsely furnished as well. Although the walls were covered with floor-to-ceiling bookcases, even above and below the window, Anna's meager possessions now occupied only two shelves.

Anna scanned the spines of her books for something relevant, but her scholarship had been in the culture of the Eastern European Vikings, the Varangians, and not American history. Anna sat at the desk. Her notebook was open to the last entry in her Longborough account:

Doctor Strickland, Jack Barnes, and the woman from the Exotic Tea and Spice Shop had all been Utgarda in disguise. The real Strickland was an elderly man. Jack Barnes, the notorious Wellersberg nightclub operator, claimed no knowledge of the Exotic Tea and Spice Shop, which did not and never had existed behind the House of Delights Chinese restaurant.

Anna closed the notebook and opened another. In it, she wrote her recollections of the dream. She described the Mesoamerican city, and Brian Teplow's iconography, the walkways floating over the stagnant lake, and the giant, long-nosed crocodiles in it. She noted the small, degenerate people with the large, pointed ears and large eyes, the Draunskur, and the Pointees of Goh-Bazh in the crowd. And she listed Sobak as the prisoner of a giant crocodile man, the old English archaeologist Cornelius Lyton, and her adversary Wolfram von Juntz, a German archaeologist. Anna then considered the other sensations. There had been the persistent smell of dead foliage and the ever-present darkness and gloom,

Anna was intrigued. Even though she had not been real, and they had only met once, the memory of Sobak, the little sister of her alter-ego, Nygof the Spy, still weighed on Anna's emotions. The girl had been devoted to her older sister, and truly heartbroken at Anna's departure. For the first time since she had cloistered herself in her home, Anna was moved to action.

After dressing for the season, including a thick wool sweater, a long wool coat, a scarf, hat, and gum boots, Anna leashed Cletus and stepped out the front door. The top of the two steps to the ground were now even with the height of the snow. Cletus pulled Anna off the stoop and she sank up over the top of her boots. She cursed under her breath as cold dampness permeated her stockinged feet.

The damage done, Anna forced herself to ignore the discomfort. She plodded across the small front yard as Cletus led her to the gate. The sidewalk on the opposite side, as well as the street, had been cleared, and once on solid footing, Anna took charge and walked Cletus purposely toward the Reister University campus a few blocks away.

The intermittent neighborhoods were residential. The two-story Victorian homes were nearly identical. Most of the residents worked for the university or rented rooms to students. With attendance down at the university, several of the houses were currently vacant, though their *For Rent* signs had been taken down to deter squatters. Nevertheless, the Wellersburg Police were patrolling the area more frequently to evict illegal occupants.

Anna had not offered her spare rooms, either for rent or for pity. She saw the lines waiting outside in the cold for the soup that the Salvation Army provided, and people standing forlornly on the street corners begging for change, but she had not been moved to altruism in spite of her unusually good situation. She tried to keep a low profile. This was aided by her dated wardrobe and a minimal use of cosmetics. But her good standing and air of purpose made her financial stability apparent to the unfortunates, who regarded her with either envy or contempt.

Anna was far from defenseless, but she had had to prove her mettle on more than one occasion when ruffians had demanded her valuables. After third encounter, Anna had taken to bringing Cletus with her when she left the house. The presence of the big, black , muscular dog deterred any further attempts.

They walked briskly. Cletus had a short coat and did not like the cold. He did his business in a snowbank along their way. Generally, he was laid back. At home, he spent most of his time laying at Anna's feet or sprawled against her in the bed. Anna welcomed the dog's warmth. Cletus seemed to recognize who Anna accepted and gazed warily at those she showed reservations toward.

Cletus barked in his deep voice as they entered the Faculty Dining Room. Eliezer Feldman, Director of the Reister University Library and Chairman of the Longborough Foundation, stood at the sound and gestured for Anna to come to the table, where he sat alone. Anna complied, and before she sat, Polly, the waitress, set a bowl of water on the tile floor for Cletus, who sat and accepted Polly's pats on his flank.

"May I have —" Anna started to say tentatively.

"Dr. Rykov will have two poached eggs, some bacon, hashed browns, and black coffee," Feldman interjected. "And bring some sausage patties for the dog." Before Anna could react, the waitress stepped away toward the kitchen.

"I can order for myself, thank you," Anna said indignantly.

"In your condition," Feldman replied, "I doubt you should be making any decisions." He scrutinized her for a moment, and then added, "You look terrible. Are you feeling well?"

"I am feeling perfectly fine," Anna replied. "But I had a very strange dream." Anna related the events of her jungle adventure over her breakfast. Feldman sat and listened silently, sipping his tea, considering the tale. When Anna produced the slip of paper, the librarian's eyes went wide.

"And you say the Englishman's name was Lyton?" he asked, seemingly oblivious to the paper.

"That is correct," Anna said with confusion. "Why do you ask?"

"It just so happens that a Dr. Cornelius Lyton, an archaeologist from Oxford, will be coming to see me this afternoon."

"What is his area of study?" Anna asked.

"Dr. Lyton has done extensive fieldwork in British Honduras regarding Mayan iconography."

"And why is he coming here?"

"He didn't say in his telegram, simply that it is on Foundation business."

"Very curious," Anna said, then put her finger on the paper. "But this is what concerns me right now. How did it get in my pocket? It was not there when I went to sleep, and I had never seen this symbol before it appeared in my dream last night. And what of Sobak? How does my fictional little sister fit into this?"

Chapter 4

March 9, 1930

Feldman continued considering Anna's dream while she researched their expected guest. They waited for him in Feldman's office at the Reister University Library.

"You said that the settlement you witnessed was dedicated to a giant crocodile man?"

"That is correct. And his soldiers were human-sized crocodile men."

"Well, as you probably know, Sobek, with an E, was an Egyptian god with the body of a man and the head of a crocodile. Perhaps your subconscious linked the two names and put them together in your dream."

"Perhaps," Anna conceded, "but that does not explain this symbol, which is not in an Egyptian style, nor how it appeared in my pocket." She thought for a moment, and then added, "And the Egyptian god had the body of a man and the head of a crocodile. The being in my dream and its minions were actual bipedal crocodiles."

Cletus put his head in Anna's lap, a gesture of concern intended to distract her when he sensed that something was bothering her. Anna rubbed gently between his eyes, by now an unconscious response, and the dog thumped his tail loudly against the table.

"Lyton has been in the field for almost nine years," Anna noted. "But he has not published anything in all that time."

"My contacts at the Royal Society said that they had presumed him lost. They have had no communications from him since 1923. Several people sent to find out what happened to him never returned. He made contact a few months ago to arrange for a return to England. Claimed he had never seen anyone searching for him."

"You have no information as to why this British archaeologist wants to see you?" Anna asked before sipping from a glass of water.

"I'm afraid not. His telegram was rather cryptic. It must have cost a small fortune from the Yucatan."

"He is coming here from Central America?" Anna said, swallowing the water in her mouth before she sprayed across the desk. She collected herself. "I had assumed that he was somewhere in the United States already. Where did he dock?"

"Lyton didn't convey his travel arrangements. The telegram arrived here yesterday evening." Feldman pulled the sheet from his desk and handed it to Anna. The message had been sent from the British Government House in Belize City three weeks earlier.

DR E. FELDMAN
LONGBOROUGH FOUNDATION
WELLERSBURG, NY

URGENT MATTER. NEED SPECIAL TALENTS. ARRIVE BY NOON TRAIN WEDS 3/10/30.

DR C. LYTON

Something nagged at the back of Anna's mind. How did Lyton know exactly when he would arrive in Wellersberg? It was unlikely that every leg of his journey would be on schedule, even if he made all of his connections.

Something was very odd about this fellow.

Anna's assessment of their visitor was correct. She started when Cletus emitted a low growl. The round, balding, older man she had met in her dream had appeared at Feldman's door, dressed in a suit of scraps and patches in mismatched colors and fabrics, and a derby hat. Anna had to contain herself lest she break out in laughter, but the dog bristled.

"Dr. Feldman," the man said in an unusual English accent, wary of Cletus' hostility, "I am Dr. Cornelius Lyton of the Royal Society." Feldman glared at Anna, and then stood and met the man at the door.

"Eliezer Feldman," he said. "At your service. And this is Dr. Anna Rykov." Lyton paused for a moment, as if frozen. Then he regarded Anna coldly, almost clinically. He dropped the duffel bag on the floor with a thump and sat in Feldman's other guest chair.

"Your costume is most distinctive," Anna said, still fighting to stifle her amusement. "I hope that you were not attempting to be unobtrusive." The newcomer did not seem to understand her comment.

"I have traveled a long way," Lyton said with irritation, after a moment, "by a most circuitous route, to avoid detection by a most dangerous adversary."

He turned to Feldman and was about to speak, when Anna said, "Are you referring to Wolfram von Juntz?" At the mention of the name, Lyton stood and backed himself into a corner. Cletus rose in response, and Anna tightened her grip on his leash. Lyton froze, and then glanced from Cletus to Anna to Feldman and back to Anna.

"You are in league with him aren't you?" he said in disbelief.

"I have no knowledge of him," Anna said, "aside from both you and he appearing in a dream of mine last night. In it, you and I were allies against von Junzt. I had shot him and was in pursuit."

Lyton seemed to gaze through Anna for a long moment. It was almost as if she was speaking a different language and he had to interpret what she said. Anna and Feldman held their positions and waited, studying the man in return. Then the Englishman slowly returned to his seat, wary of Cletus.

"What do you know of von Junzt?" he asked.

"I read in one of the journals," Feldman replied, "that Dr. Wolfram von Juntz, an archaeologist representing the German Thule Society, had discovered the existence of a prehistoric civilization that had occupied the Yucatan Peninsula before the Mayans."

The Hunter in the Shadows

"What is so noteworthy about that?" Anna said flatly. "There were many tribes in that area before the Mayan supremacy there."

"Von Juntz claims" Feldman said with a theatrical flourish, "that the evidence that he found suggests beings that preceded the dinosaurs."

"Surely he must be referring to Neanderthals. It is widely believed that they hunted for mammoth and competed with the saber-toothed tiger."

"From what I've uncovered," Feldman continued, "Von Juntz believes he found the remains of reptilian beings that existed in the Paleozoic era, four or five hundred million years ago."

During the conversation, Lyton sat quietly, observing the other two intently. It gave Anna an uncomfortable feeling that Cletus sensed. Finally, Anna stood, holding Cletus back, and confronted Lyton.

"Why are you here!" she demanded. The newcomer did not immediately react to Anna.

"I could ask the same of you," Lyton finally replied. He turned to the librarian. "Dr. Feldman, why is Dr. Rykov, and that animal, present for our conversation?"

"You mentioned in this telegram," Feldman said, holding out the paper, "that you required 'special talents.' Dr. Rykov possesses such skills. Before you tell us why you sought me out, please tell us how you came to be aware of the Longborough Foundation for Ethnographic Research? We've only been in existence for a few months."

"We have common acquaintances," Lyton replied after a furtive moment.

"Who?" the librarian countered. Lyton froze again as if dazed.

"It is best that they remain anonymous, for their own safety," Lyton responded.

Feldman was not satisfied, but did not pursue the matter. "Dr. Lyton, what can the Foundation do for you?" the librarian asked pointedly.

◆

The Englishman stiffened at Feldman's direct question. Again, he froze for a moment before responding.

"To begin with, I am not Dr. Cornelius Lyton." Anna braced herself to respond to anything unfriendly. Cletus responded to her tension with a low growl. "That is to say, this is the body of Dr. Cornelius Lyton, but the intelligence with whom you are speaking is not."

"You are claiming to be something that has possessed his body?" Feldman said with skepticism.

"Exactly," the Englishman replied, seemingly oblivious to the librarian's tone. "Mine is a race of scholars who travel through time and space learning about the multiverse by exchanging our own bodies back in our time with those beings whose existence we wish to study." He eyed Cletus nervously. "Please contain your animal. I would not wish my host's body to be damaged."

"Why should we believe you?" Anna said.

Lyton froze again. When he revived again, he looked at Anna appraisingly.

"You are the agent of the Junazhi," he said. "You are the one who released Utgarda." Anna hid her surprise.

"How could you possibly know about that?" Feldman said with astonishment.

"My race shares a collective consciousness," he replied. "What one sees, all experience." He turned to Anna. "You encountered one of my kind in the astral projectionist's domain."

Anna's eyes narrowed. "You are the Ancient Enemy," she hissed.

"My kind are not in opposition to the Junazhi," Lyton explained. "Our purpose is only to learn. The Junazhi seek to hoard knowledge. We exist at cross-purposes."

"But you steal the lives of those you 'exchange bodies' with," Anna spat. "Your method may be temporary, but your subject still has no choice."

After his usual momentary pause, Lyton said, "While it is true that we do not ask for the consent of our guests, the Collective does not suppress their consciousness and steal their bodies. We place our own bodies in their care, and offer them access to all that we have learned over countless millennia."

"How do you select beings to swap with?" Feldman queried.

"The subjects must bring themselves to our attention." Lyton froze again, this time for an extended period. Anna and Feldman glanced to each other. When he again was present, the Englishman said, "In the case of your species, our guests have been scholars of advanced mathematics; what you might call magic."

"Or occultists," Feldman added, pausing to consider this. "Why do you pause before you speak?"

"I am in contact with the collective," Lyton replied, "but my communication with them experiences a delay across the time and space between us. I have consulted the collective consciousness in order to respond to your queries."

"So you exchange minds with individuals involved with the occult." Anna was concerned, "which we consider to be dangerous, and share with them secrets otherwise beyond their access."

"Interesting," Lyton said. "Your response to this free exchange of information is to suppress it." He paused again, and then said, "I see. You believe those who pursue such inquiries to be beyond your species' acceptable norms of behavior."

"We call that insanity," Feldman said pointedly. "And in most cases, people who pursue the occult arts have motives contrary to the wellbeing of our species, our world, and or our universe. One of the goals of the Longborough Foundation is to investigate and address such threats."

"And that is why I sought you out," Lyton said with finality.

Chapter 5

March 9, 1930

"Before you explain yourself," Feldman said, "how should we address you?"

"We have found that being addressed as the host eliminates confusion, "the newcomer said. "I am in the body of Cornelius Lyton, so refer to me as him."

"Very well," the librarian replied.

"How did Dr. Lyton attract your attention," Anna asked.

"Cornelius Lyton was not the intended subject," Lyton replied. "My actual target was Wolfram von Junzt. He is an advanced practitioner of the magical sciences, as you call them. His predecessors have a history of such study, and the current incarnation is pursuing very dangerous researches."

"Do you mean that this man is the descendant of Friedrich Wilhelm von Junzt, the author of *Unauspreschlichen Kulten*?" Feldman said, dismay evident in his voice.

"That is correct," the Englishman's occupant replied. "But Wolfram von Junzt is not merely cataloging groups engaged in occult practices as his ancestor did. He is pursuing a line of research that will make the upcoming catastrophe even more profound."

"What upcoming catastrophe?" Anna and Feldman both said in unison.

"A disaster that will affect your entire world is imminent. Over a trillion creatures will die. Over one hundred million of them will be human. If von Junzt completes his current line of inquiry, it will be even worse. Humanity, and possibly all life on your planet, will be extinguished."

"What does he intend to do?" Anna asked.

"The consequences of his actions are not his intention," Lyton said. "He believes that he is conducting harmless research. He seeks to prove that his tribe is descended from the ancient masters of planet Earth. What he does not know is that those ancient masters were not human."

"How are von Juntz's activities dangerous?" Anna asked.

"Von Junzt recently uncovered artifacts that somehow survived millions of years and geological turmoil. These artifacts are the remains of the Xuxaax, the original, primal, indigenous species on Earth. If we are not successful, von Junzt will reveal these artifacts in Berlin in three weeks."

"What happens if he makes this announcement?" Feldman asked.

"He will acquire the attention of the Xuxaax who, live in secret at this time."

"You mean that some of these ancient masters of Earth have survived to this day?" Anna said.

"No," Lyton said, shaking his head. "They have not survived. But individuals transported themselves across time shortly before their civilization was destroyed. They were charged with constructing the means to bring the rest of their kind forward to the present."

"And their arrival would be inimical to humanity," Feldman said flatly.

"Yes, it would be," Lyton replied. "But there are other more likely outcomes that would be equally devastating."

"And what would they be?" Anna queried.

"If the Xuxaax were able to construct such a device or devices, the energy required to bring their race forward in time would be immeasurable. Even if they were to attempt to bring small groups to the present, each attempt would cause irreparable damage to space-time and likely destroy this dimension, or at least make it uninhabitable."

"What does this have to do with von Junzt?" Anna pressed.

"Once he makes contact with the Xuxaax, he will bargain with them. His political benefactors will acquire weapons and technologies in exchange for the seemingly innocuous materials the Xuxaax will need that will eventually devastate this world."

"And we need to intercept von Junzt before this contact is made," Anna stated.

"No," Lyton said, to her surprise. "We need to eliminate the Xuxaax who will facilitate this destruction."

"How do you know who, when, and where this meeting will take place?

"My kind have traveled the length, breadth, width, and height — to use your terminology — of the multiverse and experienced the potential outcomes of all possibilities. We know the identity of the being that von Junzt makes contact with."

"And you know where this being is now?" Anna said.

"Yes," Lyton replied. "He is in Boston."

◆

"You seem to know all about this being," Feldman said, "so why do you need our assistance?"

"I need you to kill the Xuxaax," Lyton said simply. "You have had some experience with this kind of operation." The latter comment was directed to Anna.

"What makes you think that I can complete this task?" she said, crossing her arms.

"Don't be modest, Nygof," Lyton said. "You were able to elude numerous situations and entanglements to facilitate the dispatch of the rogue wizard Goh-Bazh. And the Xuxaax intends to sacrifice your sister."

Anna was taken aback. The visitor knew intimate details of her journey to Kreipsche, and of her fictional family. She sat in disbelief for a long moment.

"How can this Xuxaax sacrifice my sister? I do not have any siblings in real life, and Sobak only existed in Brian Teplow's imagination."

"Just as you are not the same person that the Junazhi sent to that dimension, other elements of that reality have been transported into this one. You may not know your sister's alternate identity, but she is in Boston, and she is in grave danger."

"So you are saying that Sobak, my sister in that alternate reality, is actually in Boston?"

"That is correct."

"And just as Anna did not know she was here," Feldman said, "this woman does not know that Anna is in this dimension."

"And why would this Xuxaax be interested in my shadow sister?" Anna asked.

"It knows her potential," Lyton replied.

"What do you mean, 'her potential'?" Anna said.

"You were able to alter reality in the realm of Goh-Bazh," Lyton said, "and you are the Nygof of that world now."

"So you think that I can make whatever I wish happen here now?" Anna said sarcastically. "Let me assure you that this is not the case."

"Perhaps your transformative abilities are limited here because this is your home dimension," Feldman interjected. "Whereas, since Sobak originated in the other dimension, she may have similar powers here."

"Powers that the Xuxaax could make use of," Lyton said. "There are many possible explanations for what its motivations regarding your sistetr, but the matter of prominence at this time is eliminating the Xuxaax before von Junzt can encounter it."

"And I can save Sobak at the same time," Anna said , suspicion evident in her tone. "This does not sound like coincidence."

"It *sounds* like a deliberate series of events designed to get Dr. Rykov and this Xuxaax together," Feldman said pointedly. "Could this be some scheme by Utgarda?"

"I do not think so," Anna replied. "According to Goh-Bazh, his sole purpose was to trap Utgarda in that dimension and prevent Utgarda from affecting this one. If anything, our actions assisted him."

"Perhaps the Junazhi are plotting to exact revenge?" Feldman mused. "Maybe they want this Xuxaax to deal with Anna for them"

"The Xuxaax and the Junazhi fought great wars against each other," Lyton said. "Their motivations are not compatible. The Xuxaax seek to conquer and dominate, whereas the Junazhi wish to recast all of space-time to their specifications."

"Unless the Junazhi are taking advantage of this particular Xuxaax without its knowledge," Feldman replied.

"The Junazhi are quite skillful in the manipulation of minds," Anna added. "It is not inconceivable that they might have compromised this one in some way."

"The Xuxaax are genetically keyed to oppose the Junazhi," Lyton interjected with apparent frustration. "And a Xuxaax who has survived to this time must be one of their most advanced. It is inconceivable that such a specimen could be subverted, even indirectly, by the Junazhi."

"Perhaps von Junzt is setting Anna up?" Feldman said

"Von Junzt does not know of his meeting with the Xuxaax. It is in his future. Only my kind can see possible outcomes."

"But the Junazhi exist across dimensions concurrently," Anna said.

"But not across time," Lyton corrected. "They exist at the same time across the multiverse. The Junazhi are unaware of the potential apocalypse that could happen." He froze motionless again for a long moment, then added, "The consensus of the Collective is that the Junazhi are not involved." Another pause. "But they believe it is likely that Utgarda is involved in some indirect manner, and that the Xuxaax are not predisposed toward Utgarda."

"If Utgarda is involved and somehow opposed to the Xuxaax," Anna conjectured, "then perhaps this Xuxaax's plans are contrary to Utgarda's own agenda."

"You did enable his return to Earth," Feldman said. "Utgarda could be recruiting you to foil his rivals."

"An outcome that is also beneficial to you and me," Lyton added.

"It seems that my pursuing this venture is in the best interest of everyone," Anna conceded.

Chapter 6

March 9, 1930

"Where do we begin?" Anna asked. "Do you have contacts in Boston who will assist us? Do they know where this being is?"

"I will not be coming with you," Lyton said. At Anna's shocked expression, he added, "I cannot risk causing damage to my host's body. You must locate and deal with it yourself."

"How will I even know where to begin?" Anna asked. "What does it look like? Where would it make a lair? How can I harm it?"

"Those are all excellent questions," Lyton said. "There are several things your need to know. In their natural form, the Xuxaax are bipedal and reptilian, with bulbous eyes that sit above their snouts." He paused while Anna scribbled in a notebook she grabbed from Feldman's desk.

"How tall are they?" she asked.

"The average Xuxaax is —" Lyton froze for a moment and then returned, "— about seven feet tall, and roughly 300 pounds. The weight is on account of thick, scaly, armored skin."

"They sound like your crocodile men," Feldman said.

"Indeed," Anna said without emotion. "They were featured in the dream last night with you and von Junzt"

"Really," Lyton said with rapt interest. "Tell me what you saw."

Anna and Feldman exchanged glances. She recounted her pursuit of the German, her vision of the procession, her sister's plea, and the giant crocodile man who seemed to be in charge. Lyton listened with complete focus, his smile spreading to a wide grin by the time she had finished her tale.

"Do you often have premonitions?" he asked.

"No," Anna replied with dismay. "I have never had a dream such as that before. It was very lifelike, and included smells as well as sights and textures. But no sound." Lyton froze again. "What does this mean?"

The Englishman was still for several minutes. Accustomed to this behavior, Feldman stepped out of the office and returned a moment later. Lyton had not yet stirred when a brunette co-ed brought a tray bearing a pot, three cups, a sugar bowl, and a small pitcher of milk into the office and set it on the desk. She glanced at the motionless man, and then to Feldman.

"Thank you, Bernice," the librarian said, ignoring her expression of confusion. "Please close the door." Bernice nodded and, still staring at Lyton, stepped out of the office, closing the door behind her. Anna poured a cup of tea for herself and gestured to Feldman, who nodded his thanks.

"What do you make of this?" he asked as he poured some milk into the tea.

"I did not know I was to become an assassin for hire when I went after Brian Teplow," Anna said. "Though he seems to believe that this is my profession now."

"And yet it seems as if you have been selected for this task," he added. Anna nodded with a grim expression. "How do you feel about killing someone in the real world?"

"This Xuxaax is a monster," Anna said in a tone that was clearly meant to convince herself. "It is not a person, and it should not be here," she added. "It would be no different than when we killed the Pointees in the subway that time."

"But those creatures were attacking you," Feldman said cautiously. "You were defending yourselves. This time, you would be going on the offensive, and on the word of this being." He gestured to Lyton, who still had not moved.

Anna was starting to feel pain behind her eyes. The metaphysical considerations were draining her. On the one hand, she had Lyton's version of the situation, and the reality of what he was proposing was distressing. On the other hand, the dream she had had was so vivid that she could not ignore it. And Lyton said that the woman who was Sobak was in Boston. At some level, Anna felt compelled to rescue her little sister.

◆

Anna was roused out of her musings by Lyton's reanimation.

"The Collective believes that the vision you saw was a premonition of this meeting, compounded by a psychic plea from your sister, and a presage of your pursuit of von Junzt."

"I thought that I was to go after this Xuxaax?" Anna said with exasperation. Her head was beginning to throb. "You said that this venture was to be completed before it even becomes aware of von Junzt!"

"Your vision, as you described it," Feldman said, inserting himself into the conversation, "suggests that you had been pursuing von Junzt and had wounded him. But you did find it and Sobak. Perhaps this can be taken as you hindering von Junzt's plans by intercepting his would-be benefactor."

"That would be a reasonable interpretation," Lyton said.

"What else can you tell me?" Anna said, her distress evident. She pinched the bridge of her nose to try and numb the pain.

"The pressure you are feeling is the awakening of dormant senses," Lyton said. "Such is the consequence of direct interaction with the Collective."

"Someone is invading my mind?" Anna shouted.

"No," Lyton replied calmly. "The Collective is establishing a connection that will enable it to monitor your activities and perhaps provide some guidance. You will grow accustomed to the sensation."

"I have not agreed to kill this Xuxaax for you," Anna spat, the pressure in her head becoming unbearable, "and I did not consent to aliens eavesdropping on my thoughts!"

"This conduit will facilitate a more rapid exchange of information that you will need," the Englishman said with that calm tone Anna was finding increasingly more annoying.

Anna's vision started to blur, and she closed her eyes, shakily placing the cup and saucer on the desk. It felt as if a red-hot poker was being forced between her eyes all the way through her skull. She grasped the sides of her head with both hands and squeezed. Then everything went black.

Anna awakened on a sofa in the Faculty Lounge across the hall from Feldman's office. Cletus was licking her face when her eyes opened. Lyton sat impassively on another sofa at the other side of a coffee table.

"Are you all right?" the director asked. Anna blinked a few times and sat up slowly, unconsciously wiping her face with her sleeve. She assessed her condition, and realized that her head no longer hurt.

"I think the Collective has disconnected itself from my mind," she said cautiously.

"Not at all," Lyton replied. "You were overwhelmed by a flood of information. The Collective has adjusted the flow to accommodate the limitations of your neural pathways. You have been provided access to some of what is known about the Xuxaax"

Anna pictured the giant crocodile man from her dream in her mind. Suddenly, the being changed, transforming into a variety of human and alien forms. She noticed Feldman's concerned gaze. "What has happened?"

"You froze like Dr. Lyton here," he replied. "You were completely motionless for about five minutes."

"She was in contact with the Collective," Lyton said calmly. "You pursued a broad inquiry. With practice, you will learn to seek specific answers that will come to you much faster."

"What did you learn?" Feldman asked.

"The Xuxaax are able to change their appearance," she said with astonishment. Anna focused on that notion. "They take on the appearance of beings that they... eat?! How will I be able to identify them? In her mind, a light shined on the morphing being, creating a shadow in the shape of its original form. "But their shadows remain the same after they change shape. I seem to know all about them now."

"Then you should have what you need to pursue the Xuxaax in Boston," Lyton said.

"How will I know where to find it?" Anna said, but then images of shredded bodies in alleys and other secluded places appeared in her mind. "Look for savage attacks in isolated locations," she said introspectively, nodding to herself. "I think I know how to proceed."

Chapter 7

March 11, 1930

    Sleet fell as Anna and Cletus exited South Central Station. Through the precipitation, she noticed a band of toughs gathered at the corner of the building to her left. She made eye contact with one of them, and Cletus gave a low growl. Anna turned and went to the right though she had no specific destination in mind. She needed to find a hotel and start looking through the newspapers.
    For this assignment, Anna had dressed for action. She wore a long, brown leather coat over a beige sweater and jodhpurs with black boots and a brown fedora. In addition to the .25 Beretta automatic Father O'Malley had given her, now housed in a waistband holster at her back, Anna had throwing knives in sheaths on each forearm, as well as knives in each of her boots.
    Everywhere Anna looked, she saw homeless people. They gathered in alleys and in open spaces, where collections of makeshift shelters constructed from whatever lay around, commonly known as Hoovervilles, stood. The people searched for whatever work or charity they could find. The mob of unfortunates gave way to the woman and her dog, who ignored their pleas for assistance.

When Anna rounded the corner of the terminal, she found herself looking at the tracks coming into the platforms. A patchwork of simple shelters lined the grass between the street and the tracks. And the man she had made eye contact with was waiting. Before she knew it, a short man had grabbed Cletus' leash and yanked the dog from her side.

"I'll be taking that fer ya," the large, muscular man before her said in a thick south Boston accent, "and you'll be payin' me a quarter to bring it to yer destination." Not waiting for a response, he bent to take Anna's suitcase. Instead, he received her elbow in his throat, followed by a sweep of her leg that knocked the big man onto his back, gasping. Reacting to her sudden motion, Cletus sank his teeth into the leg of the man holding the leash. The dog shook the leg until his target fell and released the leash.

"I will fend for myself," she said, picking up her suitcase. Then she noticed that the man's six companions lurked nearby. Other people in the area quickly disappeared across the rails or into their shelters.

Cletus growled ominously, his hackles raised, as Anna assessed the thugs. They were laborers, she thought. They all had workmen's builds. And all had some kind of improvised weapon. One had a length of pipe, two had pieces of scrap wood, and one had a hammer. They stared at her menacingly, but did not approach on account of the dog.

Anna heard the leader on the ground rise to his knees and she kicked him in between the legs. She caught him unawares and sent him sprawling, slipping on the slush, cupping his groin in agony. At the sight of their companion's further humiliation by the slight brunette, the others attacked.

Anna had a knife in each hand before the first crony reached her, raising his pipe like a baseball bat. She expertly slashed at his nearest arm. Blood spurted from the wound, quickly coating the pipe and his other hand. The two-foot piece of lead shot out of his hands and struck the man with the hammer in the side of the head. Anna immediately slashed at the pipe man's thigh, and he and the hammer man fell to the ground, slipping on the unstable surface like Keystone Cops.

Suddenly, Anna found herself grabbed, her arms pinned to her sides by strong hands from behind. Another man struck her in the stomach with a section of two-by-four. Anna gasped as the air was pushed from her lungs. A third man hit her on the top of her head with a board. Her fedora was flattened, preventing serious injury, but she had dropped her knives.

The short man reached for Anna's suitcase, but suddenly fell backward, propelled by the pouncing Cletus, who knocked into the man with the board. The man facing her with the two-by-four was distracted, and Anna used that instant to kick him, hoping to knock him or the man who held her down. She braced against her captor, who was as solid as a brick wall, and the other assailant was propelled into a shanty by the force of her two feet. The simple structure collapsed. Its occupant ran past Anna and out of view.

Without warning, the man holding Anna lurched forward as if struck by something from behind. He was hit several more times, and each time his grip got reflexively tighter on Anna. The short man who had reached for the suitcase rose again and joined the fray behind her. She heard the sounds of traded blows, and metal on metal. The fallen attacker rose from the ruins of the shelter, holding a short-handled shovel and threatened Anna with it as we approached.

"All right," Anna said with annoyance, "that's enough." She kicked her captor hard in the shin. In the moment his grip eased, she slipped through his arms, reached behind her, drew the Beretta, and shot blindly. The big man collapsed into the snow, screaming. When Anna rose again, the pistol was pointed at the shovel-man's face.

"Enough!" she shouted. The thug before her dropped the shovel and put up his hands. Behind her, the trading of blows continued. Anna stepped sideways, keeping the one before her in view while maneuvering to see the melee behind her.

A man in a worn army uniform was holding one of the assailants' pipes. He was sparring with two of the thugs. The short man sported two large lumps on his forehead and had lost his own weapon. The other looked to have a broken nose, but punched Anna's helper relentlessly in the kidneys, stopping only to dodge the intermittent swipes with the pipe.

Anna fired a shot in the air. The fighters stopped in their tracks. They looked to Anna, then to their fallen leader, still on the ground holding his privates, and finally to the man with his arms raised, before running off in different directions.

After holstering her pistol and retrieving her knives, Anna stepped up to the soldier, who stood bent over with his hands on his knees, taking deep breaths and wincing from pain. Cletus sat by his side, panting.

"Are you injured?" Anna asked, taking her would-be rescuer's arm to guide him to a sitting position in the snow. Blood trickled from his nose, but there were no obvious injuries.

"Nothin' I haven't taken before," the man said, then he caught a glimpse of Anna and reflexively looked her up and down. He cleared his throat. "Nothing I can't handle, ma'am," he added with heroic bravado.

Anna smiled. "I am indebted to you for assisting us with those ruffians."

"I couldn't let those gangsters pester you," he replied. "They've been preyin' on the forgotten men since the Crash."

"I am Dr. Anna Rykov," Anna said, holding out her hand. "What is your name, soldier?"

"I'm Ogden Shroud, ma'am," he replied, looking at her offered hand. Anna could tell that the young man did not know whether to shake it or kiss it. "And this is Cletus," she said with a smile as she took hold of his hand and shook it. "How shall I repay you for your heroism, Ogden?" Before the man could answer, she said, "How about if I buy you lunch?"

"That's not necessary, ma'am," Ogden said automatically, though his facial expression contradicted the sentiment.

"Please," Anna said immediately, "I insist. And call me Anna." Relief blossomed on the soldier's face.

"Well," he said, "if you insist. At least let me carry your suitcase."

"Very well," Anna replied. "Can you suggest a nice place to eat near here?"

The soldier thought for a moment, looked Anna over again, and then his face became serious.

"A proper lady, like yourself," he said, "should be protected from the riffraff out here." He glanced toward the opposite side of the terminal. "The nearest place of quality is the Ritz-Carlton by the post office, ma — um, Anna."

Anna watched the forgotten men lined up in the snow along the sidewalk. They were waiting for their allotment of soup and bread provided by the Community Federation of Boston. She could see a grim-faced, matronly woman ladling what looked like thick liquid into the tin cups they all carried.

Anna faced Ogden at a table inside a coffee shop and observed the shanty town across Tremont Street in the Boston Common. Cletus lay at their feet under the table. She mused over the notion of so many people gathered for a free meal in the park that was a symbol of American independence.

"You seem able and fit, Ogden," Anna said conversationally. "Why is it that you are not employed as a policeman or security guard somewhere?"

The man's face blanched, and he turned away for a moment.

"Jobs, uh, are hard to find these days, Anna," he said when he faced her again.

"There is more to it," Anna said in her professor's voice, her tone demanding an answer. Her companion looked down at his hands in his lap and sighed. His face was a mask of anxiety when he looked up again.

"I, uh," he stammered, glancing alternately between Anna's face and the remains of the roast beef sandwich on the plate before him, "my service record, um, doesn't measure up for official jobs like police work." He looked back in his lap.

"I will not judge you, Ogden," Anna said, reaching over to gently grasp his arm. "We all have gohsts in our past."

He looked up with curiosity at the comment. "I don't think you can really appreciate such things."

"I am sure that you saw some horrible things during the war," Anna said confidently. "I have seen battles myself." Ogden took on a look of doubt. "I was in the Ukraine during the Russian Civil War. I saw death and bloodshed. I saw more peasants kill each other supporting the different factions than I saw soldiers dying on the battlefield."

Anna's ruse seemed to work. Ogden collected his thoughts and looked around the mostly empty cafe. He moved his chair to sit adjacent to her and leaned in close. Anna leaned in as well.

"The war in France was horrible," Ogden whispered, "but what I saw afterward was worse." Anna waited for more, but the soldier was staring at the table again.

"What happened?" Anna asked. "Were you still in the army?" Cletus laid his head in the soldier's lap, and Ogden unconsciously started petting it.

"My unit was assigned to occupy Koblenz in Germany after the war ended," he said, still looking at the table. "We were based in the Ehrenbreitstein Fortress across the river from the city. We were supposed to guard the bridge across the Rhine River."

"And something happened at the fortress?" Anna probed.

"No," Ogden said, shaking his head. "We patrolled all around the castle grounds as well as by the bridge. It was thick forest, dotted with tenant farmers on the borders." He took a deep, calming breath. "I was on patrol in the woods one night when I heard the screams of several people coming from a nearby farm."

"Were you alone on this patrol?"

"I'd gotten separated from the others, but I was sure that they could hear the screams, too, so I ran to the farm." He started breathing faster.

"When I got to the farm, all was quiet. The screaming had stopped. I knew the others were coming, so I looked around for any wounded.

"I heard a scraping sound coming from the farmhouse, like furniture being slid across the wood floors. I ran over there, and through the open door I could see three people — the farmer, his wife, and one of their young sons — sitting beneath the kitchen table. I heard the sound again, and noticed the other son sitting on a chair at the far end. As I watched, his head deflated like a balloon, and then it disappeared below the table.

"I bent down to look, and there were splotchy, red, frog-like things on the floor. They were about so big," he gestured with his fingers, suggesting about ten or twelve inches. "They had a bunch of suckers, like an octopus, instead of a face, and one was latched onto the kid's thigh. While I watched, the kid slid off the chair and flattened out!"

Anna remained impassive, with an expression of interest when he paused to gauge her reaction to is story. The dog's tail thumped below the table. He glanced around, alternating between Anna, Cletus, and straight ahead for a few moments.

"What happened next?" Anna said with casual curiosity in her voice. Ogden looked at her suspiciously.

"You sound a lot like them doctors I was sent to before my discharge," he said.

"I am not a psychiatrist," Anna replied. "I am an anthropologist. I study the belief systems of different groups of people. Our meeting was entirely coincidental."

"I don't think I should say anymore."

"What if I were to tell you that I believe you, and that I have seen equally unexplainable things?"

Anna noticed that the other patrons of the cafe were giving them disparaging glances. "Perhaps we should continue this conversation in private," she said as she signaled the waitress for the check.

Chapter 8

March 11, 1930

Half an hour later, Anna and Ogden were in a room at the Ritz-Carlton Hotel. The luxurious furnishings were a stark contrast to the desperation outside. Anna reclined in a comfortable armchair and Cletus had availed himself of the couch. Ogden sat in the chair by the desk.

Anna had booked the room for a week. The concierge had looked on the disheveled soldier with disdain, casually whispering to Anna that the hotel did not encourage the hiring of "those people." In response, Anna booked a room for Ogden as well, demanding that the two rooms be adjoining.

"You said in the cafe that you had seen weird things yourself," Ogden said. "Prove to me that you're not just trying get on my good side." Anna was surprised at the man's candor, especially as she had just paid for a week's stay at an exclusive hotel, but she kept her manner neutral.

"I will be back in a moment." As she stood, Cletus perked up, but remained sprawled on the couch. Anna went into the bathroom and began removing the makeup that concealed the various scars that she had collected.

"I have encountered several alien entities in my travels," Anna said while she washed. "Most of them were hostile, and some of them caused me injury." Ogden gasped when she returned from the bathroom. "These scars I received after inadvertently summoning something from beyond." The soldier examined the round marks on the right side of her face.

"That could just be from smallpox or something like that," he said.

"Smallpox would have covered my whole body," Anna replied, "not just one side of my face. And the smallpox would not appear in a linear pattern, like tentacle marks." She unbuttoned the top of her blouse, knelt in front of the soldier, and lifted her head that so he could see her neck up close.

"Those marks are the remains of rope burns from when I was captured by a sorcerer in another dimension. These as well," she added, presenting her wrists for his inspection." The soldier was speechless. Anna took his hands and looked into his eyes.

"I have also fought the sorcerer's goat-man minions in the New York Subway." Ogden stared in disbelief. "And I fought flying tentacled mutant cultists and banished the god that they had summoned in a Manhattan church." She stood, buttoned up her blouse and returned to the armchair.

"There are many such creatures," Anna said authoritatively, "and most, if not all of them seek to directly or indirectly cause harm to humanity. I am here in Boston seeking out such a creature. A being that feeds on people and then assumes their identities."

"And why would you be looking for that?" the soldier asked.

"Because its plans could mean the end of all life on Earth." The soldier studied Anna's face.

"There's more to it," he said.

"It plans to sacrifice my sister," Anna said. "Now, I have told you about myself. Tell me about you. You said that this frog-creature had drained its victims' skins. You saw it drain the boy. What happened next?"

"Then I saw the girl." The soldier shuddered, and Anna rubbed his shoulder to comfort him. Ogden looked up at Anna and she nodded encouragingly. He took a deep breath and a drink before continuing.

"She was the farmer's daughter. Maybe ten or twelve years old. She always wore a pretty white dress with little blue flowers." Ogden stared blankly into the distance for a moment. "I had seen her on several occasions. Feeding the chickens, putting the cows to pasture and such. And I watched a frog-thing leap onto her chest. It knocked her to the floor. She screamed.

"Next thing I know, I have my rifle up and I'm shooting at the thing." Tears welled up in the soldier's eyes. "I was terrified. My aim was off. The first shot hit the girl in the head. It seemed to anger the thing, because it let go of her and hopped toward me. I fired again and again, but it was so fast. It leapt at me and I finally hit it. It exploded!" Ogden gestured with his hands. "Ka-boom! Like an artillery shell!

"I must have been thrown out the door and knocked unconscious," he said after a few deep breaths, "because the next thing I remember is smelling salts from the corpsman. The patrol had arrived, and the farmhouse had burned to the ground. As I got my bearings, I noticed that I was under guard." He paused and stared blankly at the far wall.

Cletus whimpered and leapt off the bed. Then he trotted purposefully to the soldier, sat facing him, and rested his paws on the man's thighs. The sensation snapped Ogden from his trance. He returned the dog's feet to the floor and bent down to pat his flanks. Cletus licked the soldier's face. The soldier wiped the slobber away with his sleeve and returned to his seat. He took a deep breath.

"A short time later," he continued, "Some officers arrived and questioned me about what had happened. I told them the truth, but they didn't believe me. They thought I was trying to cover something up. I was put in the stockade. A few weeks later, I was charged with murdering the family and burning down the house. They said that I had assaulted the girl since she had been the only one home, and then shot her in the head. The remains of her family must have been destroyed by the fire." He lowered his face to his hands and started sobbing. Cletus rested his face in Ogden's lap.

"And you were imprisoned?" Anna asked after Ogden accepted her handkerchief. He blew his nose. "Take a deep breath." The solider did so. "And another." He complied. After several breaths, the tears stopped.

"No," Ogden continued, "I wasn't. I was in the stockade for a few weeks, when a Major Stillwell came to my cell. He asked me to tell him what had happened. A few days later, I was taken to the hospital and diagnosed with shell shock."

"So you received a medical discharge," Anna said. Ogden nodded, but he refused to look at Anna. She took his hand. "What is it?" She examined his face and posture. "You were hospitalized when you returned home." He looked at her with an anxious expression. "There is nothing to be ashamed of." She smiled encouragingly.

"I was pronounced mentally unfit and confined to the trauma ward at the Boston University medical school with veterans who had been mentally unhinged by the war."

"How long were you there?"

"Five years, from May 1922 to March 1927."

"What happened to secure your release?"

"I don't know," Ogden said with a shrug. "I never changed my story, and they never believed a word of it. I was a model patient and never caused any trouble. I guess they figured I wasn't dangerous."

"And what did you do after your release?"

"I went home to Southie," Ogden said with a frown, "but the building my family had lived in was gone and the neighborhood was all Irish. From the moment I arrived, I knew I wasn't welcome there. They ran me off a few times. The last time, they beat me senseless and dumped me in the Roxbury Canal. I was taken back to the BU hospital, but they kicked me out after a couple of days. I think they found out who I was. In any event, I've been on the street ever since."

"It sounds like yoare quite familiar with Boston," Anna said, "and with the community of unfortunates here. Is this correct?"

"I suppose I know the lay of the land pretty good," Ogden said with a shrug. "If you need to find something, I can probably help."

"That is what I was hoping you would say." Anna gave a knowing grin. "I can certainly use your assistance. In exchange, I will provide for you for the duration of this endeavor."

"Just what is it that you're trying to do?" Ogden asked.

"I am seeking to prevent Armageddon," Anna said flatly. She wanted to gauge the soldier's reaction, and she was not disappointed. Ogden did not even blink.

Chapter 9

March 11, 1930

"How do you plan to do that?"

"There is an alien presence somewhere here in Boston," Anna explained in a professorial manner. "This being will meet with a German archaeologist and trade alien knowledge for what it needs to pursue its own goals. This knowledge will be misused by mankind and result in the extinction of humanity and possibly the entire planet."

"You say it like it's already done."

"That will be the course of events if we do not prevent that meeting." Anna looked into Ogden's eyes and said, "My mission is to exterminate the alien, known as a Xuxaax, before it learns of the German's discovery."

"What does that have to do with your sister?" Ogden asked, ignoring the gravity of Anna's statement. She concealed her surprise.

"I traveled to another dimension," Anna continued, "where I discovered that my persona there had a family, including a younger sister, that does not exist in this reality." She paused to assess the soldier's response. He continued to listen intently. "When I returned to this world, I thought that I had left all that behind."

"But that isn't the case," Ogden conjectured.

"No, it is not." Anna collected her thoughts. She was intrigued by the soldier's face-value acceptance of what she told him.

"I recently had a dream in which I saw my sister. More importantly, she recognized me, and she begged me to help her. Of course, I thought it was just a dream. But then I had a meeting with another person I had met in the dream. Someone who I did not know. This person informed me of the impending doom of our world, and that my alter-ego's sister was somehow connected to it."

"How do you know that this guy is legitimate?"

"Because the body of the person I met was inhabited by another alien, whose kind travel across time and space observing the multiverse. As I understand it, they can see probable future events, but they cannot interfere with them — directly at least. The being I spoke with has seen the future of Earth if the Xuxaax and the German make contact. That is why he recruited me to prevent that."

"So why not just kill this German?"

"The Xuxaax's own plans are harmful to humanity. If the chain of events related to meeting with the German is prevented, it will devise another means for achieving its goals. If it succeeds with its own plans, we are all doomed as well."

"And who are you to go after this thing?"

"I am part of an organization established to prevent interference with humanity. It is called the Longborough Foundation for Ethnographic Research. The cover purpose is to study different cultures around the world. It was established after that extra-dimensional incident I told you about. This is the first task that the foundation has pursued."

Ogden Shroud sat back in the chair and closed his eyes. Anna could see that he was considering all that she had told him. After a moment, he opened his eyes and stood.

"I'm going to get some sleep," he said. "Wake me up for dinner." He walked to the door, opened it, and left the room.

Cletus watched the soldier leave, and then looked at Anna and cocked his head.

"I don't know," Anna said in response, "but I think he will help us."

Anna skirted the perimeter of Boston Common, stopping only to let Cletus do his business. While she waited, Anna noticed a pair of skinny young girls admiring the dog. From their slightly worn dresses and scuffed shoes, she suspected that they were living in the shanty town that dominated the open area. The two looked at Anna hopefully.

When Cletus had finished, he looked at the girls, then to Anna, and then sat with his tail wagging. Anna glanced from the dog to the girls and sighed.

"All right," she said to Cletus. Then, to the girls, she added, "Would you like to pet him?" The girls smiled broadly, and the younger of the two ran up and wrapped her arms around Cletus' neck.

"We used to have a dog," the older girl said, "before Father lost his job."

"I am sorry for your misfortune, but —"

"Oh, no, miss," the girl protested. "We are not looking for charity. It's just that losing Princess has been especially hard on Clarabelle." She indicated the other girl.

"She is your sister?"

"Yes, ma'am."

"Where are your parents?"

"Mother and Father are out looking for work."

"And they leave you here alone."

"Yes, ma'am," the girl said defensively. "Mother has entrusted me with looking after Clarabelle, and there hasn't been any trouble."

"How long have you been here?"

"Father lost his job in December."

"Right before Christmas," the other girl added.

"Yes, right before Christmas." The older girl sighed. "Then we lost our house. We were staying in a shed down in Roxbury until the old man who owned it kicked us out." The girl scowled. "And he had that big house all to himself! You could see that half of the rooms were empty through the windows, but he couldn't be kind enough to give us shelter from the snow in his shed."

Anna was taken aback by the girl's vehemence. The old man was displaying the same attitude that she herself had shown back in Wellersburg. Privacy aside, there were people with nothing who needed shelter.

"Some people are just inconsiderate," Anna said with a sympathetic expression. At that moment, she felt uncomfortable. "Excuse me, girls," she said, "but we have an appointment." The two stepped away from Cletus.

"Thank you for letting me pet your dog," Clarabelle said.

"You are most welcome," Anna replied. "His name is Cletus." At the sound of his name, the big dog wagged his tail, leaving a furrow in the snow. The younger girl laughed. "What is your name, dear?" Anna said to the older one.

"Susan Miller, ma'am." She curtsied.

"Pleased to make your acquaintance, Susan," Anna said. "And you, Clarabelle." She choked up on Cletus' leash and he stood. "Come on, Cletus," she said, continuing toward Essex Street and the Western Union office.

◆

Anna skirted the perimeter of Boston Common, stopping only to let Cletus do his business. While she waited, Anna noticed a pair of skinny young girls admiring the dog. From their slightly worn dresses and scuffed shoes, she suspected that they were living in the shanty town that dominated the open area. The two looked at Anna hopefully.

When Cletus had finished, he looked at the girls, then to Anna, and then sat with his tail wagging. Anna glanced from the dog to the girls and sighed.

"All right," she said to Cletus. Then, to the girls, she added, "Would you like to pet him?" The girls smiled broadly, and the younger of the two ran up and wrapped her arms around Cletus' neck.

"We used to have a dog," the older girl said, "before Father lost his job."

"I am sorry for your misfortune, but —"

"Oh, no, miss," the girl protested. "We are not looking for charity. It's just that losing Princess has been especially hard on Clarabelle." She indicated the other girl.

"She is your sister?"

"Yes, ma'am."

"Where are your parents?"

"Mother and Father are out looking for work."

"And they leave you here alone."

"Yes, ma'am," the girl said defensively. "Mother has entrusted me with looking after Clarabelle, and there hasn't been any trouble."

"How long have you been here?"

"Father lost his job in December."

"Right before Christmas," the other girl added.

"Yes, right before Christmas." The older girl sighed. "Then we lost our house. We were staying in a shed down in Roxbury until the old man who owned it kicked us out." The girl scowled. "And he had that big house all to himself! You could see that half of the rooms were empty through the windows, but he couldn't be kind enough to give us shelter from the snow in his shed."

Anna was taken aback by the girl's vehemence. The old man was displaying the same attitude that she herself had shown back in Wellersburg. Privacy aside, there were people with nothing who needed shelter.

"Some people are just inconsiderate," Anna said with a sympathetic expression. At that moment, she felt uncomfortable. "Excuse me, girls," she said, "but we have an appointment." The two stepped away from Cletus.

"Thank you for letting me pet your dog," Clarabelle said.

"You are most welcome," Anna replied. "His name is Cletus." At the sound of his name, the big dog wagged his tail, leaving a furrow in the snow. The younger girl laughed. "What is your name, dear?" Anna said to the older one.

"Susan Miller, ma'am." She curtsied.

"Pleased to make your acquaintance, Susan," Anna said. "And you, Clarabelle." She choked up on Cletus' leash and he stood. "Come on, Cletus," she said, continuing toward Essex Street and the Western Union office.

◆

As Anna proceeded down the street, she came upon a crowd gathered on the sidewalk, looking into the windows of a shop. As she got closer, she noted that it was a luncheonette. The homeless people glanced longingly at the diners inside. As she and Cletus approached, a policeman blew his whistle and dispersed the crowd. He tipped his hat at Anna.

"Is it always like this?" Anna asked.

"I'm afraid so, ma'am," the policeman replied. "It breaks my heart to see so many people left with nothing," he indicated the people now milling about on the other side of the street, "but other folks have the right to go about their business unmolested."

"Indeed," Anna replied. But then she thought about the two girls in the park. They were caught in the tide of misfortune as well, and they had done nothing to deserve it. "How do these people survive?"

"Various charities — funded by good people like yourself — provide bread and soup and such, but there are only so many that they can serve, and what they get is barely enough to call a meal." He shook his head.

"I've seen a lot in my years on the beat, but it's never been as bad as this."

"I suspect that things will get worse before they get better," Anna said grimly.

"I wish it weren't so," the policeman said, "but I think you're probably right." He tipped his hat again. "Good day, ma'am."

Anna watched the policeman walk away and turn the corner. As soon as he was out of sight, she noticed the dispersed people eying her with bitterness, or perhaps envy.

Chapter 10

March 11, 1930

Anna entered the Western Union office just as a neatly dressed young man was walking toward the door.

"I'm sorry, ma'am," the man said with a respectful smile, "but we're just closing up for the day."

"I did not realize that Western Union shut down at night," Anna said with disbelief.

"There are still people here to receive messages, but we don't send them out at night, except for emergencies."

"May I ask you then to send one last telegram before you close up?" Anna smiled hopefully, and Cletus wagged his tail with a doggie grin.

"Who's a good boy?" the clerk said as he knelt down and patted Cletus' head. "Do you know what you want to send?"

"I have it written out here," Anna said, withdrawing the paper from her purse. The clerk scanned the page.

"All right, ma'am," he said as he stood and locked the door. "This won't take too long."

A few minutes later, the clerk locked the door behind Anna and Cletus again. She arranged for any reply to be delivered to her hotel.

Anna glanced into the luncheonette. The diners looked up when they noticed her, but quickly returned to their food. Her appearance did not disturb them. She entered the establishment with Cletus and walked up to the counter. A matronly waitress behind the counter shuffled back and forth, attending to numerous customers as she said, "Can I help you, miss?"

"Yes," Anna said politely. "I was wondering what quantity of sandwiches you could prepare in perhaps 30 minutes for me to take with me when I return?" The waitress stopped and took a good look at Anna. Several of the diners at the counter glanced her way as well.

"What kind of sandwiches?" she asked.

"An assortment of simple fare," Anna replied. "Nothing too fancy."

"I'll have to check with Louie in the back," the woman said, indicating the doorway at the rear of the crowded dining room. "How many would you like?"

"Let's say fifty," Anna replied evenly. "Perhaps more, depending on what you have available."

"This on the level?" the waitress asked.

"Yes," Anna said. "And I will pay for them in advance."

"Wait here." Then as an afterthought, "Would you like something while you wait?"

A few minutes later, Anna sipped Coca-Cola through a paper straw whole she sat on a stool at the counter, and Cletus rested at her side with his eyes poking over the lip of the counter, when the waitress returned.

"Louie says that if you can wait until tomorrow, he can make as many sandwiches as you want."

"I would like to take them with me," Anna replied. "What could you produce today?"

The waitress glanced back toward the kitchen. Anna followed her gaze and saw a squat man wearing a stained white apron looking back. The waitress shook her head, and the man shrugged. He turned to the side, but she could see his lips move as he counted something. A moment later, he turned back and held up six fingers.

"He says he can put together about sixty simple sandwiches with what we've got in stock." She did some calculations in her head and said, "That'll cost twenty bucks."

"That is acceptable," Anna replied with a smile. "I will collect them at —

"It's going to take a little while to prepare," the waitress interjected. She looked at her watch. "We're pretty busy right now. Can you come back around seven? It should all be ready by then."

"Very well," Anna said. She reached into her purse and withdrew two five-dollar bills and three one dollar bills and assorted change. "I am afraid that this is all I have at this time." The waitress took the bills and started counting the change. "I can get more and give you the remainder when I return," Anna added with a smile.

"That's close enough for now," the woman replied. "Let's see how many sandwiches he actually puts together."

"Thank you," Anna said. "I will come back at seven o'clock."

"I'm comin'," Orville Shroud's irritated voice said in response to Anna's knock on his door. After a long moment, it opened and the bleary-eyed soldier gazed at Anna from half-closed eyelids.

"I am sorry if I have awakened you," Anna said, leading Cletus past him into the room, "but we have work to do."

"Huh?" Shroud said with a yawn.

"I happened upon two girls on our walk," Anna said, sitting at the foot of the bed, "who have inspired me to provide food for the unfortunates in the park. Once we have gained the good graces of the poor souls in Hooverville, we will be able to learn of any strange occurrences in the area."

"What kind of 'strange occurrences'?"

"People disappearing, violent deaths, strange people lurking in the shadows. That kind of thing."

"Well ya don't need to bribe folks to hear about that," Shroud said. "A bunch o' folks from Hooverville have been killed or disappeared in the past few weeks. A couple were found all torn up. But the bulls ain't interested in homeless folk. They're too busy protecting the fat cats."

"You are saying that there has been a string of violent murders in Hooverville? When did this begin?"

"Don't know for sure," the soldier said with a shrug, "but it's been goin' on for a couple o' weeks."

"That sounds like the work of our alien," Anna said with confidence. "Get yourself together. We have a delivery to make."

Anna, Cletus, and Orville stood outside the luncheonette. It was exactly seven o'clock, but the door was locked and the lights in the dining room were out. From around the shade covering the window in the front door, Anna could see light coming from the kitchen. She knocked on the door, and shadows danced back and forth from the back room before the waitress hurried to the door and opened it.

"I'm sorry, ma'am," she said with labored breath. "We closed early to get your order together. Had to send the boy out for more bread too." She stepped aside to allow the three to enter, then closed and locked the door behind them. "Louie managed to cobble together seventy-five assorted sandwiches. They're nothing special, so no extra charge."

"Thank you," Anna said with a smile. "The unfortunates in the park will appreciate whatever we can provide for them."

"I kinda thought that's what you were up to," the waitress said. "I threw in some old fruit too. It's still good, but it won't sell before it goes bad anyway."

"You are most generous."

"Well it's just about ready. Have a seat and we'll pack it all up for you."

"You bought sandwiches for the people in Hooverville?" Orville said with dismay after the woman disappeared back into the kitchen. "That wasn't smart."

"Why not? Those people have nothing. It is the least I can do."

"Well, when word gets out that a rich lady is throwing away money on the lost souls, people will be coming out of the woodwork looking for a handout."

Anna contemplated his words. She had been impulsive, and word of the grand gesture was likely to spread quickly. She looked sheepishly at her companion. He sighed loudly.

"It's a wonderful thing to do," Orville said, "but we're gonna need to be careful. Some folks are desperate enough to do violence. Like them folks at the train station. Some of them might even be there tonight."

The swinging doors from the kitchen struck the walls to either side with a bang as the waitress and the man in the apron emerged carrying wooden produce crates overflowing with paper-wrapped bundles. They placed them on the counter and then returned for three more crates.

"Here you are," the woman said, handing the last crate to Orville. "Seventy-five sandwiches and some fruit."

The Hunter in the Shadows

"You will help us take these to Hooverville?" Anna asked. The waitress looked away sheepishly.

"Can't do that, ma'am."

"If people see that the food came from this place," the soldier explained, "they will come here begging for more."

"We can't have those people scaring away our paying customers," the waitress said, wringing her hands.

"I understand," Anna said.

"Tell you what," the waitress said with a bloom of inspiration. "You send your boy back to get the rest, and I'll wait here until it's all picked up." Anna was about to speak, when she added, "but only him. Don't send any of those other folks."

"That is most generous of you," Anna said, a little less congenially. "We will not detain you too long."

Anna juggled one of the crates while keeping hold of Cletus' leash. The waitress unlocked the door. They exited the luncheonette, and the door was locked noisily behind them.

Chapter 11

March 11, 1930

A crowd gathered around Anna and Orville as they entered the collection of temporary shelters that was the Hooverville in Boston Common. Anna sought out Susan and Clarabelle Miller, aiming to feed the children before offering the sandwiches to the adults. When they reached the Soldiers and Sailors Monument, Anna set her crate down on the steps. Her companion followed suit and then assisted Anna onto the steps herself.

"I have brought fruit and sandwiches for the children," she said loudly.

An older patriarchal man wearing a soiled but well-maintained suit emerged from the crowd and stood before Anna. His face was worn but vibrant, firm but friendly. He gazed into Anna's stern face.

"That is very generous of you, miss," the old man said in a deep, clear voice that resounded over the din of the assembly. "Do you think that this meager offering will atone for your own sins? Or do you seek penance for your own good fortune?"

"I seek neither atonement nor penance," Anna replied in a loud, clear voice. "I seek merely to offer a meal to people in need." The man's gaze was unchanged. "I came upon two girls earlier today, and their story moved me to help them. But I could not provide just for them when there are so many others in the same predicament." She appraised the old man more closely and added, "It was the Christian thing to do."

"I don't think Christ was in your heart," the man said privately to her, and then said for all to hear, "but your gesture is truly appreciated. Thank you." He looked through the crowd until he found who he was looking for. "Luke! Josiah! Gather up the children so that they may partake of this generous repast." He glanced at a pair of women in the crowd. "Edith! Rosemary! Help this nice lady distribute this fine fare."

"And what about the rest of us, Joseph?" a rough young man shouted.

"You are able enough, Enoch Wilson," the old man scolded. "The sisters of mercy provide for the rest of us. The children need this more than we adults do. And as you can see, there is a limited quantity here. Barely enough for them."

Anna glanced to Ogden, who had remained at the periphery of the gathering, and nodded discretely. Her companion disappeared into the shadows to return for the other crates.

◆

The two women the elder had called out smiled appreciatively as they distributed the sandwiches. The older one, Rosemary, inspected the children's hands and made them thank the nice lady for her generosity.

"There is an assortment of sandwiches, but I do not believe that they are labeled — Anna started to say.

"This is a wonderful thing you have done, miss," Edith added, "and the children are grateful for whatever they get. Lord knows they suffer the most."

"Yes, indeed," Rosemary said. "Out here they are truly vulnerable, both to nature and the predations of their fellow man."

Anna noticed that the woman scowled as she spoke, eying a gang of toughs lurking in the shadows at the rear of the crowd. Anna followed her gaze and noted that two of the youths were among those who had accosted her at the train station.

"What do you mean by 'predations of their fellow man'?" she asked as she made eye contact with one of the two. The man disappeared into the crowd.

"Idle men have evil thoughts," Rosemary said, "and women aren't their only prey. The young and the aged are equally victimized."

'Victimized how?!"

"You don't want to know, miss," Edith said, shaking her head. "Desperate men do evil things. Even to children."

"A dozen people have disappeared in the recent weeks," Joseph said, pulling Anna out of earshot of the gathered children. "Of course, some of them just ran off, but four men were found, their bodies torn up like they'd been attacked by animals. The women and the children are just gone."

"Maybe they were taken in by some kindly folks like yourself," Edith said, inserting herself into the conversation, but it was clear from her tone that she did not believe her own words. "Your man's back," she added, indicating Ogden, who had returned with another crate.

"Tell me of these disappearances," Anna said to Joseph as Ogden appeared at her side. The old man glanced at the two appraisingly.

"No good deed goes unpunished," the old man said quietly. "I knew this wasn't just Christian kindness."

"The sandwiches are just that," Anna countered. "The plight of those girls moved me to action. But my reasons for being in Boston at this time are dire. These attacks may be related to my interests."

"What are these interests?" the elder said suspiciously.

"She's here to vanquish evil and prevent Armageddon," Ogden said. The other two glanced at him in alarm. His outburst had drawn attention to them. Ogden glanced about sheepishly.

The three stood for a few moments until Cletus, who had been sitting at Anna's side, suddenly leapt into a clump of children and rolled onto his back, tail wagging. The crowd turned to watch the dog's antics.

"I am here to locate and dispatch an evil presence," Anna said to Joseph. "I don't expect you to believe me, but it is the truth."

"I do believe you," the elder said. "I could tell that there was something about you, about both of you, that was beyond the mundane matters that we must attend to. After the rest of us eat, I will collect some people who can perhaps provide you with some breadcrumbs."

Half an hour later, Anna and Ogden stood near a fire burning in a metal trash can in an alley off an adjacent street. Joseph and Rosemary had gathered some others who they claimed had knowledge of the disappearances.

"Dr. Rykov here —" Joseph started to say to the crowd.

"Anna, please," Anna said.

"Er... Anna is investigating something that may have to do with your missing or departed loved ones. Please tell her what you can of anything strange or unusual that you have seen before or after your kin disappeared." A din rose as many of the assembly spoke at the same time. Joseph silenced the crowd with a wave of his hand. "One at a time, please." He scanned the faces and stopped at a young woman holding a sleeping baby in her arms. "Mary, let's start with you, then go around in a circle."

The indicated woman glanced around at the others nervously. Anna could tell that she was more afraid of speaking than in what she had to say.

"Anything you can tell us may save lives," Anna said. "Please share what you know. Every one of you wants us to succeed in locating and dealing with this menace."

Bolstered by Anna's entreaty and encouraging words from the others, the woman took several breaths and collected her thoughts. She glanced at Anna, who nodded with a smile, and addressed the crowd.

"My Emil went out one night to find Virginia here something to help keep her warm. When he didn't come back after an hour or so, I got worried. I thought maybe them hooligans set to him." The color drained from Mary's weary face. "But no hooligans did that to Emil. They found him the next morning ... in ... pieces." She started to sob. "At least we think it was him. It had Emil's clothes on."

One of Mary's neighbors put an arm around her to comfort her. Mary looked into the man's face. He smiled and nodded. Mary composed herself and straightened.

"What can you tell us of the attack," Anna asked the crowd. "How was the... poor Emil found?"

"He was a horrid sight, ma'am," another man said. "I found him. Emil was a coworker of mine at the plant." He took a deep breath. "His body was all scratched up, and it looked like something had taken large bites from him." Mary fainted. The man comforting her caught her, and a woman took the baby, who woke and started screaming.

"Thank you, folks," Rosemary said. 'Take them home now. What has to be said probably won't ease her troubles." She turned to the man who had been speaking. "Go on, Ed. You got any more?"

"Just that them bite marks was on his head and chest. The arms and legs was scratched up, but that was probably from fighting back."

"Do you have any idea what might have attacked him?" Anna asked.

"It were a bear," another man shouted with certainty. "I seen bear attacks before an' that were one fer sure!"

"There ain't no bears in Boston," a woman said scornfully. "Unless maybe it got away from the zoo."

"It was a monster," an old woman said. "A fell beast sent from Hell to torment us for abandoning the word —"

"Will you be quiet, Maggie!" another man said. "Your bible-thumping isn't gonna get us any closer to the bottom a this." He shook his head at the woman and then turned to Anna. "All the attacks was the same. Heads and guts torn up. Innards missing."

"Were there any tracks or footprints in the snow?" Ogden asked. "Any trails to follow?"

"The snow was packed down, and there were what looked like big bird tracks once," another man said. "Three claws forward and one back like this," he approximated the appendage with his hands, "and about that big. We followed 'em, but they disappeared once on the street."

"So the creature did not fly away," Anna conjectured. This impressed the crowed, who made sounds of surprise and agreement. "And a creature with feet that size would be… You said the prints looked like those of a bird… Then it must have been perhaps five feet tall. Are you certain that you are not exaggerating?"

"No, ma'am," another man said, and some others near him grunted in agreement. "We seen 'em too. They were about that big and in pairs about two feet apart." A thought bloomed in his head. "At one point it must have started running, because the steps grew farther apart." He gestured to his colleagues, who glanced at each other and then spread out down the alley perhaps ten feet from each other. The onlookers gasped.

Anna considered this information for a moment. The onlookers muttered quietly to each other.

"The attacks were always at night?" Anna asked. A murmur of agreement was the reply. "And you said that the snow around all of the victims had been packed down so as to clearly reveal these bird-like prints?" Again agreement. "Were the attacks in high-traffic areas?"

"No, ma'am," one of the men who had pursued the tracks said. "They was off the beaten path. Most of 'em in the trees or behind drifts. But they was clear enough." More murmurs of agreement from the crowd.

"Then I suspect that the ground was compressed by a tail," Anna said confidently. "A reptilian tale, like that that of a crocodile."

"There ain't no croc-diles in Boston, ma'am," the woman who had previously admonished the bear advocate said politely. "And don't reptiles need heat to even move around? I've seen snakes in the summer, and they're a might sluggish when it's cool."

"Where you seen a snake?" someone asked with disbelief.

"That ain't important!" the woman snapped. 'What matters is that it's too cold here for a giant crocodile to attack folks at night." Heated conversation rose from the group. Joseph and Rosemary tried to regain control, but it was a loud, anguished female voice that cowed them.

"What about the missing?!" she cried.

Chapter 12

March 11, 1930

"You've gone on at length about the dead," the older woman said with a raised fist, "but what about the missing?" The crowd split before her as she approached Anna and stopped directly in front of her. "You're looking for the thing that did the killing, but no one cares about all those folks who just disappeared."

"We can see the dead, Helen," Joseph said in a sympathetic tone, "but there's no way to know if other just ran off—"

"My Angela didn't run off!" Helen shouted. "She was taken for some evil purpose. I can feel it in my bones."

"When did this happen?" Anna asked. "Tell me all about it."

Helen's anger melted into worry as she absorbed the sincerity in Anna's voice. She lowered her fist and started ringing her hands. Anna put a reassuring hand on her shoulder.

"Angela wasn't the first girl to be taken," Helen started quietly. "She's quiet and shy, not like them other girls."

Anna nodded encouragingly.

"She's been gone almost three months."

"What does she look like?" Ogden said. Helen jumped at the soldier's voice. "Excuse me," he said "What does Angela look like? What was she wearing?"

"My Angela is just eighteen years. She's small. She's has black hair and brown eyes, and was wearing a long-sleeved white dress."

"When was the last time anyone saw Angela?" Joseph asked the assembly. A din of voices rose. Joseph cleared his throat and looked at one man. "Efrem, you first."

"I remember seeing Angela over by the fountain one night," the young man said. "She looked like she was talking to someone out of view. She had a shawl on over the dress. She was worried about whoever she was talking to."

"When was that?" Helen asked.

"It was on the night of that last full moon," Efrem replied. "I remember because whoever she was talking to was in one of the only dark places that night."

"Did anyone else see Angela that night?"

"I remember her asking about a lost child," a woman said. "Yes. She was looking for Frances McCree. The girl turned up a little later, but I don't remember seeing Angela again."

"Did the killings start before or after the disappearances?" Anna asked. Again, there was a murmur among the small gathering.

"The first body was found about a month ago," a man said. "That was Leroy Rainey." Sounds of agreement rose.

"Then there was Gilbert Meldrum," another voice said from among the crowd.

"That was about a week later," Joseph added.

"When did the people start going missing?"

"As I said," Joseph replied, "people come and go from Hooverville all the time. But the first person to leave family behind was Jessica Hilliard. That was just after the snows first fell in November."

"Tell me about her," Anna said.

"Jessica was a forward gal," Rosemary said disapprovingly. "She was a wild one. Pretty and outgoing. She was the one the boys chased. Though they didn't have to chase very hard —" Rosemary cut herself off abruptly.

"So she was friendly and outgoing," Anna said, "and probably likely to approach someone new or who she found interesting."

"You could say that," Rosemary said evenly. "More likely the strangers came to her. Always dolled up and trying to dress trendy."

"I am getting a picture of Jessica," Anna said. "What does she look like?"

"She's about your size," a young man said to Anna, "with dark hair cut short like yours." He glanced to another man near him. "And she has a nice figure."

"Come to think of it," another woman in the crowd said, "Marie Roush looks a bit like you too."

"How so?" Ogden asked.

"She was also small with short black hair," the woman said.

"What of the missing men?" Anna asked.

"All of the missing ones are young women," Helen said flatly. "That's why the coppers don't care. They think they took up as whores."

"And all the dead are men?" Ogden conjectured.

"Most of them," Joseph said. "Four of the five attacked were men. Ella Hughes escaped before her attacker could do her in."

"May I speak with Miss Hughes?" Anna asked with urgency.

"She hasn't spoken to anyone since that night," Rosemary said. "She's been in the hospital ever since."

"What can you tell us about Ella?" Anna asked the gathering.

"Well," Joseph said, "she matched the description of the other two. Small, dark hair cut short, young, pretty."

"Ella's da tough one," an older woman with a thick accent said. "She were fendin' off dem young bucks b'fore she were twelve year. A beauty she were." The woman wiped away a tear. "Not no more. That beast done tore away half of her face."

"So Ella could defend herself," Anna said in a supportive tone.

"Yea," the weeping woman said. "My Ella were good at fisticuffs, and not afraid to kick or butt with her head."

"So," Anna said, looking at the notes she had been making, "we have three men, Emil, Leroy, and Gilbert, who were all found dead in the vicinity of Hooverville, and Ella, who got away. And all appeared to have been attacked by a giant, clawed, bird-like beast." She flipped some pages. "Then we have Angela, Jessica, and Marie. They are all small women with short dark hair."

"Don't forget Katie Haskins," a voice said.

"Who is Katie Haskins?" Anna asked.

"Katie was another free-spirit," Joseph said before Rosemary could reply. "She went missing after Marie and before Angela."

"So we have four missing women, and one wounded woman," Ogden said, "who all seem to resemble Anna, and three dead men."

The Hunter in the Shadows

The alley erupted in unintelligible chatter. Anna gave Ogden a covert glare with her eyes, and then raised her hands to calm them.

"We have identified eight people whose fates may be related," Anna said in a commanding tone. "What else can you tell us? Have there been any other strange or unusual events in Hooverville? Or people lurking about who do not live here? Any wild or feral animals seen in the area?"

"Cain Dickson's been seen around," a voice said.

"Who is Cain Dickson?" Anna asked.

"Cain Dickson was asked to leave Hooverville," Joseph said.

"A sick pup that one!"

"Good fer nothin'!"

"Satan were too good for him!"

"Cain Dickson was asked to leave Hooverville," Joseph repeated, "because he was disruptive, rude, and ill-mannered."

"How so?" Ogden asked.

"He leered at the women and behaved inappropriately with the children. He was caught tempting some little ones into seclusion. The police took him away, but he's been seen around now and again."

"How does Dickson's story coincide with the attacks and disappearances?" Anna asked. A muttering from the crowd was silenced by Joseph with a gesture.

"Cain was arrested after Emil and Leroy were found, but before Gilbert." Joseph sought and received agreement from his neighbors. "The police said that Cain was the murderer, but Gilbert was killed after he was taken away, and his remains were mauled just like the others."

"And this fellow has been observed lurking around Hooverville recently?" The assembly made affirming noises. "Then I would like to meet him. Let us know the next time he is seen."

Chapter 13

March 12, 1930

Anna waited in the lobby of the First Precinct. She had been sitting patiently for over an hour after requesting to speak with Detective John Halley, who the residents of Hooverville identified as the investigating officer for the deaths and disappearances there. Anna watched as the desk sergeant glanced her way periodically after answering the telephone.

While she waited, she reread the response to her telegram from Dr. Feldman. It confirmed that Ogden Shroud had served in the American Expeditionary Force in France, and later in Koblenz, Germany. Shroud had been given a medical discharge, but there were no additional details. Feldman indicated that his various sources had been unusually uninformative when he had pressed for additional information.

So what Shroud had told Anna was partially true, but Feldman's sources did not confirm the more fantastic aspects of his tale. Something about the soldier inclined Anna to trust him. He had been truthful and helpful so far, and showed no signs of ulterior motives. But he could be adept at concealing his true self, either through training or as a consequence of whatever he experienced.

The Hunter in the Shadows

"Dr. Rykov?" a squat, muscular man in a neat, pinstriped suit said with an Irish accent. "John Halley," he added, holding out his hand. Sergeant Flynn said that you had asked to speak with me."

"That is correct, detective," Anna said, rising to her feet and grasping his hand so tightly that he winced. "I have been waiting for some time while your sergeant confirmed each time you called him that I was still waiting. I do not appreciate such treatment." She released his hand, and the detective unconsciously shook it to ease the pain. "Where can we speak in private?"

"We can go to the Chief of Detectives' Office," Halley replied, following Anna as she walked purposefully toward the stairs behind the sergeant's desk. "He's out today," he said as he caught up to her. "Right this way."

A few minutes later, Anna sat in a comfortable chair at a coffee table while the detective fetched her some tea. She had worn a conservative, skirted suit for the meeting so that the detective would not discount her on account of her femininity. She had noted the coffeepot in the kitchen, but asked for tea to keep the detective off guard. Her initial assessment of the man had been correct. He was a weak man hiding behind the authority of a badge. He had probably done as little as possible with respect to the Hooverville incidents, possibly under direction from his superiors. She needed to keep the upper hand if she was to learn anything from him.

"There you are, miss —" Halley said, offering Anna a cup and saucer.

"Doctor Anna Rykov," Anna said as she glanced at the coffee table. The detective set it down before seating himself on the chair across from Anna.

"Yes, of course." He was clearly nervous. "Um, what can I do for you, Dr. Rykov?"

"I want to you to tell me all that you know about the gruesome murders of three men and the disappearances of four women in Hooverville. You were assigned to investigate all of these crimes. I want to know everything about them."

"Well, um, I'll have to check the files and —"

"Do so!" Anna commanded, "Or take me to them and I will review them myself."

"I'm afraid I can't give you the files —"

"Then tell me what I want to know! Now!" Anna produced a notebook from her purse. "Start with a man named Emil Wilson."

"Oh, um, well, yes. Emil Wilson was an out-of-work carpenter. He and his family were living in Hooverville after the Hughes furniture factory closed."

"This I know," Anna spat. "Tell me of his murder. What evidence was collected? Who did you speak to? What were your conclusions? Get on with it!"

"Um, er, as I recall, he was the victim of an animal attack."

"An animal attack? In the center of Boston? Among a crowd of people! Poppycock!" Anna scribbled rapidly in her notebook. "How did you validate this conclusion?"

"The evidence was plain. He'd been slashed and bitten, and, um, partially eaten."

"By that, you mean that his internal organs were missing. And yet his arms and legs, the usual targets for predators in the wild, were unharmed, save for defensive wounds."

"Well, yes, the attack was suspicious for those reasons, but there was no cause to suspect otherwise."

"Tell me about Leroy Rainey."

"The Rainey case was similar. He was slashed and bitten, and his innards were missing."

"His internal organs," Anna interjected. "Specifically, his brain, liver, heart, and kidneys. Did you know that these very organs have been the ultimate goal for tribal warriors around the world for centuries? They are believed to bestow the one who eats them with the spirit, vitality, conviction, and health of the victim."

"Really?"

"And I understand that you arrested Cain Dickson for both of these crimes."

"Yes," the detective said with renewed energy, "that's right. Dickson was picked up based on the testimony of character witnesses in Hooverville."

"But he was not convicted?!"

"There wasn't any evidence to support charges of murder," the detective said, deflated, "but he was charged with lewd behavior."

"And then Gilbert Meldrum was killed in the same manner, with Cain Dickson again seen loitering around Hooverville at night." Anna give the detective a disdainful look. "And what of the missing women?"

"People have to fend for themselves —"

"Do not tell me that these three women, four if you include Ella Hughes, entered into a life of prostitution or just wandered off. Two of them," Anna consulted her notes, "Jessica Hillard and Marie Roush,

The Hunter in the Shadows

were known to be gregarious and possibly lascivious, but Angela Connor was shy and quiet, while Ella Hughes is said to be private and quite an assertive woman."

"It's not uncommon for downtrod —"

"No woman will voluntarily enter such a life! Even under the most dire circumstances. Most of the time, the women are forced into sexual servitude by domineering men who coerce them into it." Anna scowled. "All of these women disappeared after Cain Dickson was released. Do you not think the man has changed his methods after being caught? I find the lack of proper investigations most distressing," Anna said as she rose, "and I will make my thoughts known to people who will see that things change!"

Without another word, and before the detective could react, Anna walked briskly out of the office and down the stairs.

◆

When Anna emerged from the stairwell into the lobby of the precinct she was immediately grabbed by the arm, hustled into a nearby interrogation room, sat in a chair before a table, and and cuffed by her right arm to a table. The man who had brought her into the room stood behind her, but she could hear as he went through her purse.

Before her was another man. This one was in his early thirties, with short, black hair, carefully groomed. He had sensitive eyes, which were contradicted by a serious demeanor. He wore an expensive gray suit, and his blue-and-red-striped tie was crisp with an expertly tied knot. He was reading from a file when Anna entered, and he glanced at it and then at Anna several times before he spoke.

"You are Tatyana Trevena?" he said without looking up.

"Yes —," Anna replied, but was interrupted immediately.

"Why did you change your name to Anna Rykov?" he said, still focused on the file.

"And who are you to detain me and ask such questions?"

"You are a Russian national, correct?"

"I am a naturalized American citizen."

"Yes," the man said flatly, "by marriage to another Russian living in New York."

"That arrangement was made by my parents!"

"They sold you for passage to the United States." Anna saw that the man was trying get her to lose her composure.

"Such arrangements were commonplace in the old country," she said calmly, "and Fyodor Rykov was also a naturalized American citizen."

"The records at the time of his entry into the United States were not as thorough as they are today, and his citizenship can be retroactively revoked with justification."

"And why would you go to such trouble?" Anna said with irritation. "What have I done to merit this treatment?"

"You studied at Columbia," the man continued, ignoring Anna's annoyance, "but you went back to the Soviet Union to do your fieldwork. While you were there, you had several visits from the NKVD. Why were they so interested in an archaeological expedition?"

"The NKVD was suspicious of Americans in their territory. The dig was sponsored by Columbia —"

"But the lead archaeologist was a Russian," he glanced at the file, "Aleksey Sergeyevich Uvarov."

"Yes, this is correct."

"And Aleksey Sergeyevich Uvarov had been previously barred from entry into the United States as a suspected NKVD agent."

"I know nothing of this," Anna said, still annoyed. "Professor Uvarov is the foremost authority on the Varangians, who were the subject of my thesis."

"Was," the man said, looking up for the first time. "He was executed by the Soviets for sedition a few weeks ago." The man was looking to gauge Anna's reaction, but she maintained a practiced, neutral expression. "You are not surprised by this information?"

"Conditions in the land of my birth are precarious. That is why so many wish to leave."

"And, of course, being a Jew, like Marx and Trotsky, was especially perilous for you in the Soviet Union," the man said pointedly. "You would have done anything to get out. Like marrying an old man for entry into the United States to establish yourself as a sleeper agent."

"That is preposterous!"

"And yet," he said, throwing a handful of photographs and papers onto the table in front of Anna, "we have photographic evidence and witness statements suggesting such activities."

Anna examined the "evidence." There were several photographs of her in New York City with the gangster Mickey Elder and his dominatrix colleague Rose. There were also photographs of her with Harry Lamb and the vagrant Ganon, who had turned out to be Lamb's commanding officer in the Great War.

She noted a signed statement from Felix Wilkinson, Administrator of the Oak Valley Sanitarium, where the spiritualist Brian Teplow had been confined in secret, among others. Wilkinson swore that he had been coerced by Anna and her colleagues to divulge protected doctor-patient information, and that she had had knowledge of the gangsters who had brought Teplow to his facility.

"You have been documented consorting with known criminals, intimidating officials like Detective Halley, and conducting strange and disturbing researches." He closed the file with a snap. "Cease your inquiries into the Hooverville situation, and your involvement with Ogden Shroud."

"You know what is happening, you do not want it to stop, and you do not want me to bring attention to the situation. Who are you, and what do you know of these events?"

"I am J. Edgar Hoover, Director of the Bureau of Investigation." He paused to let that information sink in, but Anna's expression remained neutral. "You have no business pursuing this matter. Leave it alone or the Bureau will look into your affairs more closely."

Hoover nodded, and he and the other man left the room, taking Anna's purse with them.

Chapter 14

March 12, 1930

Suddenly, Anna was overwhelmed by a feeling of vertigo, swooned, and laid her head on the table. She was dazed. Had they drugged her somehow? No. Her mind had been suddenly flooded with images and information. What she received were images of J. Edgar Hoover heading the Federal Bureau of Investigation, as his organization would ultimately be called, through years of glory and infamy while collecting secrets used to blackmail the rich and powerful. At the same time, she saw Hoover exposed as a homosexual and ostracized, ultimately taking his own life. And she also saw Hoover arrested and imprisoned for abusing his power.

Along with the imagery of Hoover, she saw Ogden Shroud being committed to an asylum for the shootings in Germany and eventually dumped on the streets of Boston. She also saw him summarily executed for the events at the farm. And she saw Shroud promoted to an officer on account of his experience and serving in a principal espionage role in another war against the Germans. Anna reasoned that, in her bewilderment following the interrogation by Hoover, she must have inadvertently sent a flood of inquiries to the collective.

The Hunter in the Shadows

Another volley of images entered Anna's mind. This time she saw herself carefully rise and make her way discretely out of the police precinct. She also saw herself locked in an asylum and forgotten. And she saw herself back in Brian Teplow's world as the dutiful elder daughter, with Sobak and her family in their home. Anna realized that the first of the three images was the best outcome.

She slowly sat up. The vertigo came, but subsided quickly. Anna pulled a pair of pins from the cuff of her jacket sleeve and picked the lock of the handcuff. Then she rose to her feet and waited a moment until she felt stable. Then she padded quietly over to the door.

Through the frosted window, she saw no signs of movement on the other side. She tried the handle, and the door was not locked. Taking a deep, centering breath, Anna opened the door and stepped confidently out into the hallway. As she rounded a corner, Anna saw a side exit from the building. She walked casually up to it and out into an alley. The door closed behind her, and she noted no handle on the outside.

She walked carefully down the alley, away from the front entrance. She took a circuitous route back toward the Ritz-Carlton, but as she approached the front entrance from the south, a heightened awareness alerted her to several young men, of similar build and in similar suits and hats, arrayed strategically on the block by the front entrance.

No sooner had Anna spotted the agents staking out the hotel than she was grabbed by the arm and pulled into the coffee shop she had visited the previous night. She turned to see Ogden Shroud holding a duffel bag. Instead of his uniform, he now wore an old corduroy jacket over faded overalls with the collar of a faded, red flannel shirt peeking out, and a black watch cap. Shroud led her deeper into the shop, out of view of the front window.

"I saw some of those guys in the hall," the soldier said quietly, "and they looked like trouble. They went to your room and started looking around, so I hightailed it out of there." He handed Anna the bag. "I don't know what you did, but those G-Men aren't being too subtle about their interest in you."

"Mr. Hoover himself told me to abandon my inquiries into the events in Hooverville," she looked pointedly at her companion, "and to part ways with you. I suspect that they know of what you saw in Germany, and they have classified it as a military secret."

"Well, they know about your interest in the strange things going on, and they know what you look like, so you'd best change into the stuff in the bag. It'll help you blend in better on the street." Anna looked in the bag.

"Where did you get this?"

"It was donated by the some of the folks in Hooverville. They're prepared to hide you among them so you can continue your investigation. They're watching Cletus now." He pointed to a door in the back of the shop. "You can change in there."

When Anna emerged again, she had been transformed. She had replaced the skirted suit with a pair of worn and patched men's trousers, a long-sleeved flannel shirt, a stretched-out sweater, an over-sized, worn, wool jacket, and fingerless cotton gloves. She had wrapped a kerchief around her head to conceal her hair and knotted it in the front. Lastly, Anna had adjusted her makeup to be more subtle but still conceal the scars on the right side of her face.

"That should do," Ogden said, eying Anna up and down appraisingly. Noting that she was carrying the duffel bag, he said, "Leave that. You won't be able to wear those things anymore." He guided her back toward the rear of the shop. "Out the back door."

As they crossed the room, Anna noted their image in a mirror hanging on a wall. She looked quite different. Poor, but not like she had as a child in Russia. She looked American. And in their matching attire, she and Ogden looked like just another young couple overcome by the financial collapse.

◆

The two returned to the tent colony from the north, the opposite direction from the Ritz-Carlton. They could hear laughing children before they caught sight of the Soldiers and Sailors Monument. There, they found the young people chasing Cletus around the marble pillar, enjoying the big dog's random changes of direction.

"I thought seeing him running loose would make the G-Men think you had abandoned him," Ogden said.

"That was a good idea, but they know I am investigating the deaths here. They will keep this area under surveillance." She scanned the immediate vicinity, but did not see any of the similarly dressed young men. "We had best get into hiding until after dark."

"This way," the soldier said, taking Anna's hand in an intimate manner.

At first she was surprised by his forwardness, but she realized that his gesture was for show to establish their new personas. She let the young man lead her through the crowd. Many of the women judged her with their gazes. Despite her attempts, Anna still appeared to be in better condition that those around her. However, Anna noted when some of the women recognized her and distracted their neighbors to allow the pair to disappear into the shanty town.

Shroud led them to a collection of scrap wood, cardboard, and some bricks that turned out to be covering a deep hole dug into the snow. Inside the makeshift shelter, Anna saw Rosemary and Joseph arranging the small space. By the light of an oil lantern, she could see six sleeping areas, as defined by piles of blankets and straw. The two farthest from the entrance, and least visible, appeared to be of recent construction and unoccupied.

"You can stay here as long as you need," Joseph added. "We'll lead anyone looking for you away."

At Rosemary's beckon, the newcomers examined the spaces laid out for them. To her surprise, beneath a thick pile of blankets for her was an old, but serviceable mattress. Shroud examined his space, but there was only straw beneath his covers.

"This is too much," Anna protested. "Surely you or your neighbors need these things more than I do."

"Don't look a gift horse in the mouth!" Rosemary said with matronly severity. "You're not accustomed to the chill like we are, and you don't have them warm clothes anymore. You'll be lucky not to catch cold out here."

"Thank you for your consideration," she said sheepishly and laid down in the bedding to try it out.

"It's the least we can do," Rosemary said. "Them Federals don't care about us. But you do, and we thank the Lord for bringing you to us."

"And what of Cletus?" Anna asked with sudden anxiety.

"He'll be just fine," Joseph replied calmly. "He's been adopted by the children and seems to be able to fend for himself."

"I hear he's been looking around for the best place to bed down," Rosemary added with an unexpected grin, "and the kids are competing to make him feel welcome."

"We've told them to keep him away from here, but he'll be nearby when you need him," Joseph added.

"Very well," Anna said. "It seems that we are your guests at least until nightfall. However, we need to make some preparations."

"What do you need us to do?" Joseph asked.

Chapter 15

March 12, 1930

Darkness, and the temperature, had fallen when Anna emerged from the makeshift shelter. The shanty town was illuminated by the lights of the surrounding buildings, but the drifts of snow and the trees created a pattern of light and darkness that left great areas of shadow among and around the shelters.

The gloom of the wet chill, which suggested more snow soon, was amplified by the doleful silhouette of the full moon, which was barely visible through the low-hanging clouds that also obscured the tops of the tall buildings. Anna shuddered and pulled her thin wool coat tighter around her. She was given a cloche hat by one of the women when it was evident that she was not adapting to her new circumstances well.

In the intervening hours, Anna had outlined her plan, which was to capture and question Cain Dickson. Joseph had recruited a dozen men and women from Hooverville to keep watch for their former neighbor, with instructions from Anna that they were not to approach him. They were to patrol in pairs, and if Dickson was

The Hunter in the Shadows

spotted, one was to keep him under surveillance while the other informed Joseph or Rosemary, who in turn would tell Anna inside her shelter.

Anna did not tell the residents of Hooverville that the man they had seen was not Cain Dickson, but a Xuxaax in disguise. The monster was searching for women who resembled her, and killed the men to cover its tracks. When it was found, Anna and Ogden would follow the creature to its lair and deal with it there.

That had been the plan, but after several hours inside the cramped enclosure, her muscles had become stiff, and she found Ogden Shroud uncomfortably close. In spite of the hot stew that Rosemary had prepared just outside, the damp chill penetrated her clothing and seeped into her bones. Once it was dark, Ogden had persuaded Anna to stay inside, practically blocking her exit from the shelter, but eventually she was so cold that she needed to move to get her blood flowing and crawled over the soldier. He wrapped his arms around her and pulled her close

"I have not said anything until now," Anna whispered in his ear, "but you should not assume to take such liberties with me, even with the best intentions." Then she squirmed out of his arms and exited the shelter.

In the wan light of the nighttime landscape, Anna was indistinguishable from the other people around the tent city. Suddenly she was knocked down from behind and landed face first in a snowbank, but was quickly flipped onto her back by a wet muzzle that licked the snow from her face. Cletus sat next to Anna, leaned in against her, and wagged his tail. His furry warmth was a welcome relief.

"Don't be so obvious," Anna mock-scolded the dog. "You'll give my cover away." She scratched his ears and ran her bare hands over his wet, fluffy coat. Cletus woofed once as Ogden emerged from the covered hole in the ground. He pat Cletus' flank, and then pulled Anna to her feet.

"Don't sit in the snow," he admonished in a whisper, "It's a sure sign that you're not from around here." He looked around and then added, "No one else is sitting in the snow. They know that if your clothes soak through, they'll be wet until spring." He patted her body down front and back to brush off the snow without consideration for where his hands went. Anna noticed that several people were watching and took hold of his wandering hands.

Their embrace was interrupted by Cletus, who interposed himself between the two and separated them. Several of the onlookers laughed and returned to their own affairs.

Anna noticed Helen, mother of the missing Angela, staring at her. She stepped over to the woman.

"In the moonlight," the old woman said, "you're the spittin' image of my girl." She wiped a tear from her face, and Anna took hold of her shoulders.

"We will find out what has happened to her," Anna said with confidence. "We are only just beginning our investigation."

"I just hope them Federals don't scare that good-fer-nothin,'" Helen replied.

"I do not think that they would deter him, if he is what I think he is," Anna said.

"What do you mean by that?"

"I just mean that we must have hope," Anna said, realizing her blunder, and embraced the woman.

Helen's concern evaporated when Cletus again appeared and separated the two.

"He sure looks out for you," Helen said, stooping to speak to Cletus face. "You keep her out of trouble, now," she said, patting Cletus' head.

"We need to stay together," Ogden said as he put an arm around Anna's shoulder. "You can't run off like that. If the G-Men come after you, I can lure them away so you can escape. But not if you wander off."

"Your man has your best interests in mind, too, honey," Helen said. "You would be wise to listen to him."

Before Anna could say anything, the older woman ducked into her own shelter.

"That is what I am talking about," Anna said to Ogden as she removed his arm. "People think that we are a couple."

"What's wrong with that? You fit in better as part of a couple than by yourself. Look around — there aren't any unattached women here."

Anna realized that her companion was correct. She had not seen any unescorted women in Hooverville. Even the older teenage girls were in the company of a man, if not in groups when in the shanty town.

"Very well," she conceded reluctantly. "But do not get any ideas about making our 'relationship' more intimate."

"What's gotten into you?" Ogden asked incredulously. "I have done nothing but look out for you since we met!"

"And just what do you expect in return for this generosity?" Anna gave him a knowing look.

"That's not fair!" he protested. "Sure, you're pretty and all, but that was the last thing on my mind out here!"

"But it *was* on your mind. Don't you wish to 'share my bodily warmth'?" she cooed as she leaned up against him. She could see that he was getting frustrated. "Until it becomes absolutely necessary, hands off!" she said and walked off toward Joseph, who was warming himself by a campfire.

◆

Anna pulled her jacket tight and wrapped her arms across her chest to stave off the chill. She had survived the cold winters of her childhood in Russia, but she did not recall the damp chill present tonight.

Joseph looked up from rubbing his hands together at the sound of Anna's footsteps in the snow.

"Has there been any news?" she asked.

"Not yet. But it's early."

"Helen said that I resemble her daughter Angela. Is this true?"

"Dressed like that," he replied, appraising her appearance, "there is a strong similarity."

"I suspect that Mr. Dickson may be looking for me."

"But why are you looking for him?"

"I believe he is holding my... step-sister captive." Joseph regarded Anna intently.

"Why would a lowlife like Cain Dickson be interested in you, or even know who you are?"

"I do not believe that he is who he appears to be." Before Joseph could inquire further, Anna asked, "What were the girls doing out alone at night?"

"From what I've heard, Angela was the only one out for a specific reason. She was looking for Frances McCree. Don't know why the others were out. But as you heard, most of those girls were libertines."

"I am going to wander over past the pond as if looking for the dog." She looked toward Charles Street and a densely forested area. Then she whistled, and Cletus appeared out of the mist. "He has made his presence here quite apparent. It would not be unreasonable for someone to look for him in the dark." She patted the dog's head.

"Go hide," she said to the dog and pointed toward the indicated collection of shadows. Cletus ran off, leaping through the snow. Anna feigned surprise, shouted, "Cletus come back!" in her best American accent, and plodded through the deep snow after him into the secluded darkness.

Chapter 16

March 13, 1930

    The snow drifts in the northeast corner of Boston Common climbed up to Anna's thighs, and her movements were slow and deliberate. Cletus had leapt through the snow, creating a furrow of sorts, but it was only a small respite. She could feel the cold wetness seeping down from under the legs of her pants into her work boots. Once under the cover of the trees, the drifts sank down to below her knees, but the going was equally slow on account of the shadows and low-hanging branches.

    "Come back here," Anna scolded, concealing her accent as best she could. After fifteen years in New York, she could approximate Brooklyn English well enough, but she did not know if that would fool her prey.

    As if on cue, Cletus bounded out of the foliage and ran around Anna several times, just out of reach, before disappearing back into the shadows. Anna feigned exasperation and followed the dog's trail into the snow-covered branches.

    Suddenly, both of her arms were grabbed by strong hands, and she was pulled bodily out of the foliage onto Beacon Street Mall, the wide path that was illuminated by a streetlight at the top of the embankment that surrounded the perimeter of the park. Anna was momentarily blinded by the light, but her vision quickly cleared to find that she was being held by one of the men she had seen watching the Langham Hotel earlier.

"Kind of late to be out yourself, miss," the man said as he set her feet on the ground. He retained his tight grip on her arms and examined her face in the light. "Who are you and what are you doing here?"

"I'm looking for my dog," Anna replied in her American accent. "He ran off this way."

"What is your name?" When Anna hesitated in responding, the man gazed at her face again. Anna saw the recognition when he noticed her scars. He reached into his coat to pull something out.

Whatever he was reaching for snagged on the coat, and when his gaze turned from Anna to the pocket, she lashed out and struck his throat with her fingertips. The man fell to the ground, gasping for breath, and Anna ran down the path followed by Cletus.

As she approached the steps that led up the embankment to the street, Anna noticed a pair of the athletic young men in suits and overcoats at the gate to the sidewalk. She ducked into the foliage. There was no indication that the men had spotted her.

The copse turned out to be thin, and Anna found herself on another path heading back toward Hooverville.

Anna meandered through the maze of shelters, taking a circuitous route to Helen's shack. The old woman was surprised when Anna entered unannounced, but Anna's anxiety was evident.

"What's happened?"

"One of the government men identified me. I disabled him, but they will be looking for me. I need a change of clothes."

"Take what you need," Helen said, pointing to a stack of folded clothing sitting on a long-vacant pallet. Anna pulled off the wool coat and slipped on a long, faded, blue cotton coat. Helen plucked off the cloche hat and put her own wide-brimmed black bucket hat on Anna's head.

"That should do," Anna said, adjusting the hat. In the distance, she heard a policeman's whistle. "I had better get away from here now. But do not worry. I will find Angela."

"I'm praying for you," Helen replied, clasping her hands. "Good luck."

As she emerged from the shelter, Anna saw the lights of several people marching toward the shanty town from the direction she had come. She stepped calmly but quickly through the assorted hovels in the opposite direction. When she reached the other side of Hooverville, Anna noted a group of policemen armed with flashlights and pistols approaching from the entrance by the Metropolitan station on Lafayette Mall. She turned back and made her way through the growing crowd of residents awakened by the commotion, watching another group coming from the intersection of the Beacon Street and Charles Street Malls. She slipped into the trees.

Branches and brambles raked her face and twice plucked the hat from Anna's head before she found the open area around a bandstand. Across it, Anna could see more men at the Boylston Street and Tremont Street exits. To the left, beyond the bandstand and through some trees, she could just make out the forms of men near a monument. To the right, across the Ball Field, she saw more of the agents and policemen near the exit at the intersection of Boylston and Charles Streets. If she left the cover of the trees, she would be seen by her pursuers.

Suddenly, a scruffy-looking man's head popped up from beyond the snow drift around the bandstand and gestured urgently for her to join him. Anna could hear the noises of the agents and policemen approaching from several directions. She glanced to the man, who now pointed down below to his right and mouthed, "Good hiding spot." He then indicated to approach from his left around the piled snow.

"There's the dog!" a voice shouted to her right, and the sounds of movement approached her position.

Anna had forgotten about Cletus, who must have followed her scent. There was nothing she could do about him now. She scanned the immediate area. The group that had been near the monument ran past her position toward where the voice had come from. As soon as they were out of view, Anna ran to the bandstand, noting that a path had been dug in the snow to a door just below the level of the snow. The scruffy man waved her over, and then ducked through the low door. Anna followed into the close chamber, noting that the shadow cast on the floor was that of a bipedal humanoid with a long muzzle and thick tail, just before the door closed behind her with a thud.

In an instant, Anna whirled around, but the knives in her sleeves caught on the cuffs of the cotton coat, which were tighter than the wool one she had been wearing. She sensed an incoming attack and dodged to the side. She struck the rounded wall of the dark, low space and fell to a crouch, pulling one of the knives from a calf sheath.

Her eyes were slowly adjusting to the dim light in the room. She saw movement and rolled to the side. Something heavy swept over her and hit the wall where she had been a moment before. She grabbed the object and tried to stab it repeatedly. The surface was thick and scaly, and her blade did not pierce it.

Suddenly, Anna's shoulder was pierced. There was a sharp, burning sensation, and then Anna was paralyzed. She dropped the knife as her fingers straightened. Her muscles would not respond to her commands.

"You might be the one," the scruffy man's rasping, sibilant voice said. The door opened, and now Anna saw one of the agents instead of the scruffy man who had called to her. "Come," he commanded, and Anna found her legs moving on their own. She tried to speak, but her mouth would not move. She was a prisoner in her own body.

Chapter 17

March 13, 1930

When Anna and the man emerged from beneath the bandstand, a foggy mist obscured the landscape, making everything indistinct. Anna's body followed the impostor agent past the Boston Massacre monument to Tremont Street. The agents Anna had seen there previously were gone, probably headed to the site of the commotion on the other side of the park. Anna followed the doppelganger across the street, where they turned right.

They continued for several blocks before passing through a short but dark tunnel under train tracks. When they emerged on the other side, Anna's captor was no longer in the form of one of the muscular, gray-suited G-men. He had become a frail, stooped old lady. The neighborhood was now residential, and Anna found herself assisting the old woman through rows of nearly identical houses on the gloomy, deserted streets.

The crone led Anna casually to an unassuming townhouse. Rather than climbing up the five steps to the front door, the old lady led her companion down a short flight of steps to a door under the front porch.

There, she produced a key from her handbag, unlocked it, and gestured for Anna to enter.

Anna's feet took her into a low-ceilinged storage area. She heard footsteps coming from the floor above. Then the door closed behind her, casting the chamber into darkness. As her eyes adjusted, she noted two, thick-paned windows between the room she was in and the next room. At the far end of the storage area was a door adjacent to that neighboring room. She could feel warm air in coming from that direction. She had started to walk toward the door, when a scaly hand bearing five, long, clawed finger grabbed her shoulder.

Startled, Anna turned to see a stocky, reptilian being with scaly skin and a long, powerful tail. It was a crocodile man from her dream. It was the Xuxaax. Remembering that her knives had been useless against its tough hide, Anna turned and escaped through the doorway and then through another one beyond it. She ran blindly down a long hallway. The footsteps upstairs were closer now.

Suddenly, Anna saw a light at the far end of the passage coming from a spiral staircase leading upward. She headed to it and climbed the steps two at a time until she ran into something. She started to fall backward, but a strong, but gentle hand caught her.

"What have we here?" a tall, thin man said with an unnerving grin. He was young, perhaps in his thirties. His blond hair was messy, and he wore a stained artist's smock. He took hold of Anna's chin with his other hand and tilted her face up toward him and the light coming from behind him. He turned her face from side to side, appraising it. Then he noticed her scars, and grinned maniacally. "I think you might have found her this time. Put her in the garden with the others."

Anna jumped when the scaly hand, now illuminated, grabbed her shoulder from behind again. Then she felt the sharp, burning sensation as its claw stabbed her in the back of her neck and she passed out.

◆

Anna regained her senses in a greenhouse. The ceiling of the chamber was opaque glass, and the room was pleasingly warm. Among the many wide-leafed tropical plants that lined the walls were four very lifelike statues of young women in modern clothing, two on either side of a path that led to a blank wall. All appeared to be running in panic toward her, and all bore more than a passing resemblance to Anna.

Anna stood third in the line to one side of the path, but she was facing the others, and her wrists were chained together and tethered to a

The Hunter in the Shadows

ring set in a column above her head. She had been relieved of her knives, her coat, and her sweater, but otherwise appeared to be as she had remembered. She was not in any pain, save for the lingering burning sensation from the Xuxaax's paralytic poison.

Turning her head was difficult, but Anna managed to glance across the path to her left, where she could barely see another young woman in the corner of her eye. The woman was real person, not a statue, and appeared to be paralyzed like Anna. She was tied to another column in the same pose facing the blank wall at the far end.

Looking with her extreme peripheral vision was uncomfortable, so Anna faced the far wall again. She could not blink, but her eyes were not dry or irritated. She considered her situation.

If I am shackled, she thought, *there must be some risk of escaping. The paralysis must be temporary.* She considered the strange man. *He must be the one in charge, and not the Xuxaax. Perhaps Lyton had been wrong.*

Anna tried to think of escape options, but bound and paralyzed all she could think of was to wait out the effects of the poison and hope she was not harmed or injected again. Dejected, Anna attempted to clear her mind to try and sleep.

As she stood frozen — her gaze focused on the opposite end of the room — Anna noticed the wall was not blank. There were very small characters or glyphs written across the central portion of it. The iconography filled in the shape of an arch that nearly touched the glass ceiling. Unable to look away, Anna saw the writing start to move, at first barely perceptibly, and then faster and faster until there was a regular rhythm to it.

◆

Captivated by the motion, Anna's surroundings faded away, and she found herself in a chamber. Hourglass-shaped columns supported a strangely vaulted ceiling. The room was illuminated by globes set into the ceiling and filled with shelves containing what looked like rectangular blocks of metal. Spaced througohut the chamber were tables, some of which held the metallic blocks.

As she looked around, Anna noticed several other things there with her. They were all conical beings with multiple prehensile stalks near the apex at the top. Two of these stalks ended in three-fingered appendages that looked like crab legs. One stalk ended in a ball, from which cone-shaped organs periodically emerged from and retracted. Another supported a large, bulbous head sporting four enormous eyes facing in opposite directions. It was tipped with a handful of whisker-like tentacles that writhed independently. All of the creatures had metallic rings around the head stalk where it joined the main mass. Most of them also had rings around the claw stalks as well, and an arc of electricity connected them, though they did not seem to impair movement.

Anna turned to look at objects on the table. The metallic blocks had glyphs carved into them. There were also cups with what looked like carved bones in them, as well as stacks of thin metal sheets. Some of the sheets were scattered about the surface, and Anna could see glyphs that had been freshly etched into them. She reached to take one of the carved bones from the cup and realized that her hands were claws. She was in an alien body in some kind of alien library. The beings were taking the metallic "books" from the shelves with their claws and holding them up, arching their necks to look at them. They stood motionless for various lengths of time, and some of them took the bone styli, which — when touched to the metal sheets — initially glowed blue before fading into indentations in the surface.

Anna was struck by vertigo as she swiveled her head stalk around to look at her current form. The body and the stalks were corrugated and glossy, and changed colors between greens, blues, and purples in the light. Her claw stalks bore the metal cuffs. She tested them by stretching them in opposite directions and found that the range of motion was limited, with the electrical arc appearing and buzzing at a certain distance.

At the sound of the arc, another of the beings, who did not have claw-stalk cuffs, glided over to Anna.

The shackles are for your own protection, an alien voice said in her head. *You are not accustomed to our form, and it would be quite easy for you to damage your host's body.* Then it glided back to where it had come from.

Anna looked at the book on the table nearby. To her surprise, she found that should could read the glyphs, and that the book was entitled *Mental Communication Among Humanoid Species*. It described an advanced mathematical formula beyond human understanding. Anna's curiosity overcame her unexplainable situation, and she was compelled to experience the "book."

As she scanned the metal surface, the glyphs started to move. The characters were completely different from the ones in the greenhouse, and images appeared in her mind. Anna felt a strange sensation. She became aware of a new sense of perception, more mental than physical, very far away. She mentally pursued the sensation and found herself staring at stationary characters on the wall in the greenhouse.

Chapter 18

March 14, 1930

Oh god, oh god, oh god, oh god! a female voice said in Anna's head. Anna knew it wasn't her voice, but its source was nearby. She was still paralyzed, and nothing had changed in the greenhouse. Though she was starting to get uncomfortably warm, she could detect no signs of perspiration. Her entire physical being was frozen, but her mental abilities were still functional, perhaps even enhanced without the distraction of her physical needs.

Oh god, oh god, oh god, oh god! the voice said again, and this time Anna realized it was the thoughts of the woman bound to the column across the path. Anna strained to glance at her again. She was younger than Anna, perhaps early twenties, and wore a fashionable, long, plaid, wool skirt with a dark, loose, long-sleeved blouse. Her hair was a golden shade of brown.

Sobak, Anna thought, focusing on the girl described in the alien book. Of course, the paralyzed woman showed no indication of having heard her, if she even could. *Sobak!* she tried again with more intensity.

Oh god, oh god, oh god, oh god! the voice repeated. *Now I'm hearing voices, too.*
The voice you are hearing is coming from the woman tied to the other column.
What? How? Who
I have come to rescue you and kill that monster.

This is just my mind trying to deal with this. Standing here frozen for so long has strained my sanity.

How long have you been here?

OK, voice in my head, the skirted woman said defiantly, *I'll bite. I think I've been here about a week.*

Have you been paralyzed the whole time?

I loosen up after a day or two, but that creepy guy comes back and injects something into my neck each time.

Do you know why they captured you?

The guy told that monster that I was the key to their Great Migration, whatever that means. Who are you?

My name is Dr. Anna Rykov. I have been sent to kill the crocodile man and prevent the apocalypse. That Great Migration will be the disaster I was sent to stop.

What do I have to do with the end of the world? I'm just Maggie White.

What do you do? Anna felt compelled to ask for some reason.

I'm a photographer. What does that have to do with anything?

Perhaps nothing. Anna paused to collect her thoughts. *Maggie, I am going to tell you something that you will find hard to believe, but I want you to consider it objectively. Can you do that?*

I suppose.

You can change reality with your mind.

What?

You have the ability to change your surroundings through force of will.

Horsefeathers! And how could you possibly know that?

Because I could do the same in your world.

What do you mean in my world?

You and I are pan-dimensional sisters.

Pan-dimensional what?

We are sisters from different dimensions. I am from this one, and I was sent to yours, but unintentionally brought you back here with me.

Okay, crazy lady! Stop right there! I know who I am and I've never seen you before in my life. She paused, and then said, *and we look nothing alike!*

I know you have a past history and family that probably goes back generations, but that is all fiction. Your real name is Sobak, and you come from a land called Kreipsche that is ruled by the mad wizard Goh-Bazh

Now I know you're making this up. I was born in the Bronx and grew up in Bound Brook, New Jersey. I came to Boston to take pictures for Fortune Magazine of the effects of the stock market crash in New England.

I grew up in Brighton Beach after my parents and I came from Russia in 1914. But when I was sent to your dimension, I found that I had another name, Nygof, and another life, as well as parents and a younger sister named Sobak. When I completed

The Hunter in the Shadows

my mission there, I was brought back to this dimension, but your world collapsed, and parts of it manifested here.

Listen, whoever you are, the voice said with irritation, *leave me alone. I have enough to worry about without voices in my head!*

Sobak! Sobak!

Go away!

Maggie, Anna said, *you are the only one who can get us out of this!*

Leave me alone! the voice shouted in Anna's mind, and then the mental connection disappeared, leaving Anna with a tremendous headache.

◆

Anna tried for an unknown period of time to regain her contact with the other prisoner — without success. At some point, she must have lost consciousness, because she was awakened by pressure on her neck, where she discovered that the man who had caught her on the staircase stood before her checking her pulse. Then he reached up to examine Anna's bonds.

"We wouldn't want you breaking loose before the main event," he said with amused sarcasm. "You might turn into one of them." He indicated the statues of the women behind him, who were all in poses of panic. "They weren't the right one, but Zakraph thinks that there is something special about the two of you, and maybe we need you both.

"Numerous pantheons throughout history suggest a duality of light and dark, sun and moon, birth and death. Isis and Nephthys to the Egyptians, Freyr and Freyja to the Vikings, Yama and Yami to the Hindus, Hunahpu and Xbalanque to the Mayans, and many more as you know, Dr. Rykov."

"Yes," the blond man said with a cruel smile, "I know who you are. And I know why you are here." He turned to the other paralyzed woman. "You are here to rescue this lost Aryan bloom," he brushed Maggie's cheek with the back if his hand affectionately before it wandered over her body, "and stop us from bringing forth the rise of Germanic supremacy. But you are too late, for we will summon forth the future!" He laughed maniacally as left the greenhouse.

◆

Anna was aghast. The Thule Society was already in contact with the Xuxaax, and had been for some time. She had been sent to them, and her presence was apparently required for the ritual to bring the crocodile-man race forward in time. They would flood out of the gate, cause death and destruction, and keep the United States occupied while Germany prepared for a new war and then took over the world.

Or at least that is what the Germans thought. The Xuxaax, like all the extra-dimensional beings she had encountered, could not be trusted. Lyton had led her straight into the enemy's hands. He must have planted the images in her dream to appear immediately before he arrived to recruit her. And now she was powerless to stop them.

Or was she? They needed both her and Sobak to power the gate. If one or both of them failed to provide whatever they needed, perhaps the ritual would not work. But the prisoners needed to work in concert if they were to thwart the Xuxaax' plan. She needed to convince Sobak to help her.

Anna focused her mind on the other woman. *Sobak! Sobak!*

Leave me alone! the voice in her mind shouted.

Maggie! I need your help! We have to stop them from opening a gate and bringing forth more of those monsters!

I am not an ancient goddess! I am not your sister from another dimension! I am just a girl from New Jersey who likes to take pictures!

You are all of those things. Anna realized that she had had god-like powers in Goh-Bazh's world, and Sobak must have those powers here. *You have the power to free us. All you have to do is believe it to be so, and it will be!*

You are insane! It doesn't work that way. Wishing doesn't make things real!

No! Anna replied, *Wishing does not make things real. Do not wish! Believe! If you believe what you want to be real, then it will be.*

Suddenly, Anna felt extreme pressure that made her want to cry out, and Anna's link to Sobak was gone. There was nothing of the sensation that the alien book had bestowed on her. Anna tried again and again, focusing on the psychic pathway that had been forged between them, but no trace of it remained.

Perhaps I should read the tome again, she thought, and focused on the runes on the far wall. But this time the glyphs remained stationary, and the sensation she had felt when the writing moved did not occur again, no matter how long she concentrated on them.

Perhaps the Collective can provide me with some assistance. Anna still did not know how she had sent her previous mental inquiries to them, but she fought back the mounting fear she felt and attempted to focus. *How do I regain communication with Sobak?* She repeated the thought over and over again, but there was no response. Either she was unable to make contact with the Collective, or they were not answering her.

Chapter 19

March 14, 1930

Some time later, the blond man and the Xuxaax, Zakraph, returned. Zakraph carried a long, smooth, golden rod in his claws.

"Well, ladies," the man said, "it's almost time. Soon, I, Conrad Fox, will open the way and the tribe of Zakraph will flow through. The new world order will arise, and the Aryan race will deal with the lesser races." He looked at Sobak and said, "Any last requests?"

As he reached to fondle her frozen form, the crocodile-man raised the golden rod up to place it into sockets in the two pillars and that faced each other. Fox grabbed one of its forearms and dragged it down.

"Not yet," Fox said. "We need to test the mono-polar pathway first. If one can establish the gate, we'll see how strong it is. If she burns out, we will still have the other one. And if the way can be established, then we will insert the other and hopefully strengthen it." He released the monster's arm.

"You see," he continued, "The previous subjects were not suitable. Zakraph detected some potential in them, but it was insufficient. We tried four times adjusting the configuration, the inscriptions, and the incantations, but each time, the life force drained away and they were petrified." He indicated the statues along the path.

"But then the runes suggested that a more powerful subject was nearby. Zakraph purused the aura and we found you." He cupped Maggie's chin. "We thought you were the key, and while you have been more resilient that the others, my calculations suggest that even you alone would not be sufficient for our purposes." He released her and turned to Anna. "What a boon it was that you, of all people, Dr. Rykov, should show up on our doorstep!

"Your aura is nearly visible to the enlightened eye." He tapped the middle of his forehead. "With your 'sister' to establish the gate, your life force should be more than adequate to keep it open." He admired her form with a lustful grin. "And if you survive, you will serve me in other ways."

"Come, Zakraph," Fox said as he stepped back to admire his involuntary subject with a satisfied grin. "We should give them some time to recover before the ritual begins."

Sobak! Sobak! Anna shouted mentally, but there was no response. *Maggie! Speak to me!* She sensed an emotional paralysis preventing the other woman from speaking. *Maggie! That was part of the ritual he spoke of. It was intended to steal your will. You cannot let him take control of you! You cannot let him win!*

This is too much for me to take, a meek voice croaked. *First, I'm hunted by a monster. Then I'm frozen like a statue in this hothouse. Then I'm talking to voices in my head. And now I've been menaced by Dr. Frankenstein. This can't be real! It can't be!*

It is only as real as you believe it to be. You can change this reality. You can free us and banish those monsters!

I can't. It's not possible. This isn't real. This isn't real. It can't be.

Then the link was broken again.

◆

Anna was revived from sleep by a loud snapping of fingers in her ear. She could tell by the light growing through the glass ceiling that morning was coming when she. Her arms ached, and Anna realized that she was no longer paralyzed. Instead, she hung painfully by her shackled wrists from the ring above her. She opened her eyes with a start, peering up the muzzle of the crocodile man and into his bulbous eyes.

"You are not like the others," the monster said in a whispering, hissing voice. "You have power, and you have been sent to prevent the arrival of the Xuxaax. But this world is ours, and we will reclaim it."

The Hunter in the Shadows

Just then, Conrad Fox entered the chamber, dressed in gold-trimmed ceremonial robes that reminded Anna of the ones that Goh-Bazh had worn. He walked behind Anna and slapped her rear hard. When Anna jumped with surprise, he said, "Good. Your paralysis has lapsed. Now we can begin."

"Begin what?" Anna croaked. Her throat was parched.

Anna cried out as her head was painfully pulled back by the hair and Zakraph held her mouth open, Fox poured a beaker of milky, green fluid into her mouth. Anna gagged on the thick liquid, and she tried not to swallow, but lacked the strength to spit it out. Fox then emptied a large glass of water into her mouth, forcing the vile fluid down along with the welcome liquid. The artist released her hair, but the monster then forced her mouth closed and held her head back until she swallowed.

"That's better," Fox said, returning to Anna's view. He carried an easel bearing a covered canvas that he set down before her. Then he pulled off the cover with a flourish. The image was of her and Maggie, paralyzed and bound to the columns, their clothing in disarray as two of the crocodile men fondled and ravished them. It was incomplete, but Anna could see that both of the women in the portrait bore expressions of ecstasy. "What do you think? It's early yet, but I think I've captured the scene rather well."

"What has happened?" Anna spat. "What have you done to us?"

"Nothing has happened to you," Fox said with distaste. "Not yet, at least." He turned to Maggie and cupped her chin in his hand. Anna noticed that she was also not paralyzed, but that she was gagged with a leather bit that had a tube extending from it, and runes similar to those on the far wall had been drawn on her exposed skin. She screamed through the gag at his touch. "This one, however, will serve exquisitely."

Fox grinned sadistically as he pushed the tube into the leather, and, as Maggie started to gag, Anna realized that he was pushing it down her throat. Then he stepped behind her and wrapped his arms around her waist. The monster then stepped up to her and Fox turned her body until Anna saw her in profile. Maggie's eyes widened in terror as the humanoid reptile inserted the exposed end of the tube into the roof of his mouth, and Anna could see something pass through it into hers.

"What are you doing to her!" Anna shouted.

"We're preparing her for the ritual," Fox said in a lackadaisical tone. Maggie's eyes seemed to glaze over, and her body went slack, suspended by her wrists. Fox released Maggie and removed the device from her mouth. Stepping up to Anna, he wiped the length of the tube with his thumbs before handing it to the crocodile man. He then took Anna's cheeks in his hands, stuffed both of his sticky-sweet thumbs into her mouth, and stretched her cheeks painfully. Anna tried to kick him, but her legs would not respond. "Don't worry," he said with a chuckle at her twitchy, erratic movements, "your turn will come soon."

Fox removed his thumbs, making sure to wipe the material on the inside of Anna's mouth, and turned to Zakraph. "Let's begin. How should we start this time?"

"You are allowing this monster to conduct a ritual, and you do not even know what is supposed to happen?!" Anna said with contempt. "You are an exemplary representative of the Aryan race!"

"Silence!" Fox shouted. "What is the procedure?"

"Come," Zakraph hissed, and the two stepped out of Anna's view. "Do as I do," he said, and started chanting. After a few iterations, Fox joined him, standing behind her. To Anna's surprise, the artist's pronunciation of the alien syllables was very close to that of the monster right from the start.

"Xo nuj edso edo ev kxom, kxo Xuxaax Fhaojk.
Xo hicot xoho ad kxoah dumo, hicot eloh Jecjkxoam.
Rik xo tat dek johlo kxo Xuxaax, xo toleihot kxom.
Udt cabo kxom, xo joobj ke hokihd.
Oyi tatd'k kxadb kxuk Oyei noho kxo edcOy edo?
Xo nuj kxo vahjk.
Thuwed Xuxaax!"

Anna tried to speak, but she could feel the anesthetic effect of the material from Fox's thumbs numbing her mouth and throat. The chanting was mesmerizing, and as she watched, the runes carved into the very center of the arch in the far wall started to glow. At the same time, a faint pressure started building in Anna's head.

Suddenly, Anna felt a surge of electricity through her body and all her muscles flexed, her hair standing on end. In her peripheral vision, Anna could see that Maggie's body had also straightened and she was standing at her full height on her toes. At the same instant, the pressure in Anna's head grew uncomfortable. Fox and Zakraph kept droning on, their resolve bolstered as the glowing runes on the far wall expanded to a nearly humanoid shape.

The pain grew unbearable, but Anna was distracted by the feel of Fox as he pushed his body against her from behind and started caressing her arms. Everywhere he touched tingled, and Anna welcomed it as he moved down her arms to her shoulders, then up her neck to her face. Her head felt as if it might explode from the pain, but in her blurred vision Anna saw a figure emerge from the glowing arch.

Chapter 20

March 15, 1930

Anna gaped as her vision cleared in spite of the throbbing pain in her head. The figure solidified into the form of another Xuxaax striding unevenly toward her from the arch in the wall, which was no longer glowing. Zakraph lumbered toward it with a similar gait that seemed to make the newcomer defensive. The two squared off, adopting an aggressive posture and circling each other. Their tails lashed wildly, and the newcomer struck one of the female statues, sending it crashing against a side wall, where it broke into several pieces. Anna noticed that the statue was not hollow. She could see the solidified innards of the woman where they were now exposed.

Fox laughed maniacally, stepped in front of Anna, and kissed her. "It worked!" he said as he pointed to the second crocodile man. "It worked! The reign of the master race will begin soon!"

"But do you know who the master race is?" Anna said hoarsely. The two reptilian beings were now interlocked, their jaws clamped down on each other, looking like scaly wrestlers. "Perhaps they have other plans for you."

The Hunter in the Shadows

"Those things only want to return to existence," the artist said dismissively. "They don't have the intelligence or skill to overthrow the Aryan people." He paused as Zakraph threw the newcomer over his head by the tail. His opponent landed on its chest, and Zakraph mounted it. Fox smiled. "It seems we have brought our friend a mate."

"The quicker for them to reproduce and overwhelm you." Anna's voice adopted a worried tone. "Those creatures are monsters. Their only interest in you is as a means to their own ends. Once they have what they want, they will no longer need you. Or any of us."

Fox ignored her. Instead, he watched the two monsters mate. Neither exhibited any expression of pleasure or made any noises aside from heavy breathing and slapping their tails on the ground. The artist was completely fixated on the congress until he glanced about the room and disappeared behind Anna. He returned a moment later, feverishly drawing the scene on a sketch pad.

Anna glanced over to Maggie, who now hung limply from her chains. Her face was pale. Her eyes were wide, but had a blank expression. Her mouth was slack and drooling slightly, and she shivered sporadically.

"Maggie?" No response. "Maggie!" Still nothing. Anna focused on the catatonic woman. *Maggie, can you hear me?*" There was no response, but she could sense awareness in the other woman. A mental image appeared in her mind of Maggie's skull parting to show Anna pieces of her brain slowly weaving back together, one neuron at a time. *Her mind is trying to deal with the trauma.*

When Anna looked back, the Xuxaax were rising to their feet. They strode over to face Fox. Anna saw no indication of attraction or intimacy in the aliens' features. Aside from differences in coloring and scale patterns, she could not really tell them apart.

Fox moved to put a hand on each of their shoulders, but the newcomer backed away, crouched, and hissed. Zakraph towered over her so that she was in his shadow. The crouching monster dipped her muzzle in submission.

"This is Shenzosh," Zakraph said without expression As the other rose to stand defiantly next to him, Fox started to speak, but Zakraph stopped him by saying, "She will not understand you. She has not benefited from the millennia of experience I have collected. She does not even know what you are."

Shenzosh glanced at Anna and Maggie and hissed with excitement. The male monster snapped his muzzle and hissed louder. The female again dipped her muzzle.

"She wishes to eat the females. I have told her that they are mine and that she must not harm them without my permission."

Fox shrugged. "As you wish. Now that we have two of you, do we even need them?"

"We will need several more of the Xuxaax before the psychic conduits are unnecessary."

"Then let's get started," Fox said excitedly, snatching the leather gag from a table.

The male Xuxaax grabbed his hand. "We must feed Shenzosh first."

"And we'll need to wait for *her* to revive," the artist said, glancing at Maggie, "before we can use them both. Come. We'll find suitable sustenance for her in Boston Common."

Fox moved toward the door, and Zakraph followed. Shenzosh ambled over and sniffed at Maggie.

Anna focused on the alien and shouted DO NOT! with her mind. The female crocodile looked around, startled, and then followed the other two out of the greenhouse.

◆

In his excitement about the success of the ritual, Conrad Fox had failed to paralyze his prisoners. Alone in the greenhouse, as Maggie had not moved since her ordeal, Anna worked at the cuffs chained to the metal ring set in the column. They were tight and bit into her skin, but they felt like they were loosening. Her blood was lubricating them, and the return of circulation to her hands brought back some sensation to her fingers. She kept twisting her wrists, hoping that her hands would slip though the cuffs before her captors returned.

Maggie started to moan. Anna looked over and saw that her eyes no longer held that wide-eyed stare, and some color had returned to her face. The traumatized prisoner wiped her chin against her shoulder and moaned again. Anna could see by her stance that her loins were sore, but she stood uneasily to take the weight off of her wrists.

"Are you all right?" Anna asked.

"I feel dirty," Maggie said, her voice unexpectedly strong as she looked around the room. Her gaze paused on the portrait on the easel. "I had hoped that this was a nightmare and that I would wake up all safe in my bed," she shut her eyes and angled her head up toward the warm sunlight coming through the thick glass ceiling of the greenhouse, "but it seems that this nightmare is real."

"You have the ability to change things. To save us!"

The Hunter in the Shadows

"Don't start with that again! I am not your lost sister from another dimension with supernatural powers! If we're going to get out of this we have to figure out a real way to get free and escape from this hell house."

Anna was discouraged at Sobak's denial of who she was, but also encouraged by her strength of will and her focus. "So who are you, then?"

"I am Maggie White. I'm a photographer, currently working for Fortune magazine capturing images of America after the stock market crash. Who are you?"

"I am Dr. Anna Rykov from the Longborough Foundation for Ethnographic Research in Wellersburg, New York. I am an anthropologist involved in the investigation and resolution of supernatural and extraterrestrial threats."

"So you know what those monster croc-men are," Maggie stated. "That explains why you are here, but what does any of this have to do with me?"

"What I told you of my journey to another dimension was true. I had a little sister there, and I was able to alter reality and bring about the collapse of that world, which was a figment of the imagination of a disembodied brain." Anna could see that she was losing credibility. "Those beings, known as Xuxaax, are an ancient race that existed on Earth before the time of the dinosaurs. They were an advanced civilization, extinguished by some cataclysm in the distant past. However, they possessed the technology to send some of their kind forward in time."

"And they kept themselves hidden until now?"

"They possess the ability to take on the appearance of people..." Anna paused, searching for the right words, but finally said, "...that they have eaten."

"They eat people! Is that what happened to the missing men of Hooverville?"

"Yes," Conrad Fox said as he entered the greenhouse. "And then they can assume their likeness. That is how Zakraph is able to get close to his victims. But his shadow reveal his true form."

"And Ella must have seen his shadow and fought back."

"That was unfortunate," Fox said. "His baser instincts took over after his confinement by the police. He was weakened by the lack of adequate food while he was in jail."

"So Cain Dickson was his first victim," Anna mused. "And that creature used his appearance to lure outgoing young women to their deaths."

"And their would-be protectors into his belly." He smiled with malignity. "But they were essential to refining the procedure."

"And you killed Gilbert Meldrum to remove suspicion from 'Cain.'"

"I need him to bring forth the rest of his people."

"You mean to say that there are more of those disgusting things?!" Maggie said in disgust.

"There are a few scattered around the world. But through the ritual we just shared, they can open a portal to the past that other Xuxaax can pass through to the present."

"And then, with the assistance of the Thule Society cells in each of the Triple Entente powers, they will weaken the defenses of our enemies so a Third Reich can rise to rule the Earth!"

The artist went to the easel and removed the portrait, which Anna saw him put on a table at the rear of the room strewn with assorted art supplies. He selected an empty canvass mounted on a frame and returned to the easel.

"While our colleagues rest," he said, "you can watch as I create a masterpiece." He pulled a piece of charcoal from the pocket of his smock and started drawing. "It starts with a sketch like the one I drew after our new guest arrived." He made a rough sketch of the two crocodile beings mating, and then continued to explain his actions as he refined the image.

Chapter 21

March 15, 1930

Fox rambled on about techniques and artistic trends, with his back turned to the prisoners, for what seemed like several hours. He was completely focused on his painting. While he was distracted, Anna and Maggie both tried to slip through their shackles behind his back. Maggie could not work her hands through the tight manacles, but Anna's hands were smaller, and her restraints were looser.

Eventually, when the artist stepped back to admire his work, Anna struck. As soon as the German agent was close enough, Anna grabbed hold of the metal ring with every ounce of strength she possessed and flung her legs up and around Fox's thighs. She had hoped to grab him by the neck, but failed to raise her legs high enough.

Fox was surprised and fell forward, but before he could call out or hit the ground, Maggie wrapped her legs around his neck tightly.

"Do you have him?" Anna said.

"Oh yes!" Maggie said with a vicious grin.

"Hold him, but don't kill him. We need to know where the other Thule cells are." Anna released her hold, and the artist collapsed to his knees beneath the other prisoner. Then she gritted her teeth, squeezed her fingers together as tightly as she could, and let go of the ring. The pain was excruciating as Anna crouched down and pulled. Her blood-slicked hands sank slightly into the metal cuffs, but not enough.

Fox struggled against Maggie's muscular, adrenaline-infused legs, grasping them in his hands and pulling. With each tug, she squeezed his throat tighter, but her strength was waning. "I can't hold him forever!" she shouted.

In desperation, Anna simultaneously bent her legs to raise them off the floor. Gravity pulled on her straining hands. Anna screamed as her right hand slipped through the metal cuff and all of her weight transferred to the still-manacled hand, now wedged into the restraint. Quickly, Anna returned her feet to the ground and pulled the connecting chain through the embedded ring.

"Where are the keys?" Anna demanded. Fox continued to struggle against his captor, who now sat on his shoulders to relieve the pressure on her own wrists. Anna kicked the man hard in the kidney, and he straightened involuntarily. "Where are the keys to these manacles?!" Fox glanced toward the table holding the art supplies. Anna ran over to it and rummaged through the mess of rolled-up canvases, brushes, tubes of paint, cans of solvent, and other things.

Suddenly, Maggie screamed. Anna's back had been to the others, and when she turned, she saw that Fox had fallen flat, pulling Maggie down with him. Blood flowed down her arms where the manacles had bitten deeply into her wrists. Anna rushed over toward Maggie, but was thrown to the floor by a heavy weight from behind. Anna felt a sharp pain in her side as the female Xuxaax effortlessly flipped Anna onto her back and sat on her hips, lashing her tail violently and snapping her jaws.

"Kill her!" Fox shouted. "She is an American spy. She knows how to destroy you!"

"No!" Zakraph commanded as he batted Shenzosh aside. He stomped on Anna's abdomen, and in the moment she was stunned by the assault, lifted Anna to her feet by the arms, passed the chain of her manacles back through the metal ring, and snapped the cuff around her wrist again. Then the monster squeezed both cuffs, crushing them around Anna's wrists until they bit into her skin. Fox appeared next to him, holding the gag, but Zakraph pushed him aside. "We do not need that now."

"What?" Fox was surprised. "Why not?"

Zakraph pointed to the golden rod, which was leaning against a wall. Shenzosh retrieved it and thrust it into the slots in each of the columns.

The Hunter in the Shadows

The rod fit tightly, and she had to flex it in order to insert it into the holes. Anna felt an impact. The rod was in contact with the metal ring.

The two aliens then stood up against the bound women from behind. Anna felt Shenzosh's scaly paws rubbing her exposed skin. Her claws sliced through Anna's shirt and left faint lines of blood in her skin.

"What are you doing?" Fox shouted as the Xuxaax started chanting.

"Xo nuj edso edo ev kxom, kxo Xuxaax Fhaojk.
Xo hicot xoho ad kxoah dumo, hicot eloh Jecjkxoam.
Rik xo tat dek johlo kxo Xuxaax, xo toleihot kxom.
Udt cabo kxom, xo joobj ke hokihd.
Oyi tatd'k kxadb kxuk Oyei noho kxo edcOy edo?
Xo nuj kxo vahjk.
Thuwed Xuxaax!"

The aliens ignored him. Fox grabbed at their scaly hides to pull them off, but the aliens were fully committed to the ritual. Unconsciously, he was hit by one of their flailing tails and flew into the table of art supplies.

Anna was engrossed in the ritual. Her eyes were closed and she moaned softly. Unlike Fox's sensual touch, the female monster's touch was primal and erotic. Anna was being pulled into the spell physically as well as mentally. Where she had had a splitting headache previously, she was now overcome with lustful impulses.

Shenzosh had started rubbing her body against Anna's back, and once her sweat-soaked shirt had been pulled free of her trousers, the touch of the monster's belly scales against Anna's bare skin was stimulating.

But Anna was distantly aware of a commotion. The aliens continued their droning chant, increasing in intensity as the erotic sensations grew. She was aware of a growing energy around her, and then a blinding light penetrating her eyelids. Anna was overwhelmed by the smell of more Xuxaax. They roared and sniffed around her. Then other alien voices joined the chant.

◆

Anna heard a distant voice shout, "Down there!" followed by the sound of machine gun fire and faint pattering sounds from above. She immediately became aware of a wave of heat blowing in her face and activity happening around her. She opened her eyes to see a dozen new crocodile men in the greenhouse. The arch in the far wall had been replaced by a swirling blue vortex in which she could see a steady stream of the aliens approaching from the distance in ones and twos. A moist, tropical breeze, tainted by their reptilian scent preceded them.

Zakraph and Shenzosh now stood in the center of the room among three other chanters. Others were posturing, circling each other as the first two had when the female arrived. A few sniffed the shackled women with interest. The tapping sound was coming from several of the gray-suited men shooting Thompson submachine guns into the thick glass of the ceiling. In spite of the heavy barrage, it was not showing any signs of weakness.

Anna looked over to Maggie, whose screams were barely audible above the cacophony all around, and who was contorting her body to avoid the thrashing tails and probing muzzles of the new monsters. Anna focused and shouted *DO NOT!* with her mind at the newcomers. The Xuxaax again looked around, startled, and then each started posturing as if one of the others had challenged it. The shackled prisoners found themselves surrounded by monsters clawing and biting each other.

Anna felt helpless in the midst of the brawling aliens. Once she was struck in the chest by a tail, and Anna suspected that it might have cracked some ribs as she was thrust into the air. The crushed metal around her wrists bit into her flesh, preventing her from flying across the room.

As soon as she could breathe normally again, Anna realized a growing energy was rising from within her. What Anna had at first identified as tropical heat was in fact some kind of dimensional energy that she was absorbing. Anna concentrated hard on the chains binding her, willing them to release her. But nothing happened. She tried against Maggie's manacles, again to no effect.

Suddenly, the doors into the greenhouse burst open, followed by a hail of gunfire. A group of federal agents fanned out from the entrance. J. Edgar Hoover paused at the entrance to insert another drum magazine into his own Thompson. While the agents concentrated their fire on the monsters emerging from the portal, Hoover himself mowed down the chanters. The federal agents were gaining the upper hand for the moment, but more Xuxaax were emerging from the portal every few seconds.

Maggie! Anna focused on the other woman, who she sensed a connection with almost immediately. *Do you feel the energies flowing from the portal?"*

I think so, Maggie replied. *I didn't know what it was, but I can feel it flowing through me.*

We need to stop the tide of new ones. I think we can close the gate if we channel the energy in us back at it.

How do we do that?

Clear your mind of distractions, and concentrate solely on closing the gate. Can you do that?

I'll do anything to end this torment.

Do as I do. Anna closed her eyes. She pushed away the pain in her wrists, arms, and back. She closed off awareness of the sounds of battle around her. She concentrated on the growing energy pulsing through her body. Then she fixed her gaze on the glowing arch in the opposite wall and shouted, *Close the door!* over and over again in her mind.

The Xuxaax crossing through the temporal gateway began running toward the greenhouse portal as the glow of it started to pulse. Anna cast a sideways glance at Maggie to see that she was staring down the swirling blue tunnel defiantly. Anna regained her own focus and pressed harder with her mind. Then Anna's view was blocked by the face of Shenzosh, and Anna felt a scaly hand grab her face, lightly piercing both cheeks. The great maw opened to reveal a pointed tubular protrusion in the roof of her mouth aimed for Anna's forehead.

Suddenly, the monster was hurled backward, scraping a thin line across Anna's cheeks, as Cletus struck Shenzosh. The big dog landed on top of her and tore savagely at the alien. The Xuxaax clawed at Cletus, but was clearly losing the fight as Anna heard bones cracking and saw huge chunks of flesh flying from the monster's throat.

Anna glanced toward Maggie to see Ogden Shroud tear Fox away from the woman and punch him repeatedly in the face until the German fell to the ground.

Maggie! We were succeeding. Concentrate! We need to close that portal! Anna saw a nod of understanding from the other prisoner and renewed her mental assault on the glowing arch. *Destroy the portal! Eliminate everything in it!"* Anna put all of her energy and will into the effort. Her head started throbbing with pain. She felt a trickle of blood from her nose, and her vision also became tainted with a red hue, turning the portal purple. The light from the portal began to strobe faster and faster.

"Anna! Anna! Are you all right?" Ogden asked, staring into Anna's face. He tapped her cheek. Anna snarled and then grit her teeth. Ogden followed Anna's gaze and then turned away as the strobing became uncomfortably fast and bright.

Anna and Maggie screamed in unison, their backs arching, seemingly floating a few inches off the ground. Then there was a blinding green flash, the glass ceiling of the greenhouse shattered, and a stream of wintery-cold air flooded the room.

Chapter 22

?

Anna regained awareness. Once again, she was in the alien library in the body of one of the conical beings. She scanned the strangely vaulted chamber and noted several more of the entities there, but eventually she somehow knew she had found the being that she was looking for, and she knew that the body was no longer inhabited by the English archaeologist.

She manipulated her new form and glided across the octagonally tiled floor to her target. Just before she reached it, the electrical charge on the cuffs around her claw-tipped stalks increased in intensity and the three-fingered appendages were magnetically drawn together.

In the back of her mind, Anna sensed danger and betrayal. No, not betrayal. Duplicity. And the sensation was not her own, it was all around her. It was the perception of the Collective. They were aware of her presence and intent, and blamed her for the failure of the Xuxaax' plan. The being that had traded minds with Lyton turned its head stalk to face Anna. It had an aura of frustrated menace.

You sent me to Boston because I was necessary for the successful creation of the Xuxaax portal, Anna thought.

You have worked everything out, I see, the being facing her replied. *The Xuxaax were a means to our own end, and they needed the psychic energy I introduced into you through that book to initially establish the portal.*

You planted the image of Sobak in my dream, but Maggie White is not Sobak's surrogate. You left the von Junzt fragment in my pocket. Was there any validity to the von Junzt story?

Wolfram von Juntz did discover evidence of the Xuxaax in Central America. And he and his benefactors will bring about the mass extinction of trillions of lifeforms on Earth. But it will take a different path now, without the assistance of the Xuxaax, and will not extinguish humanity.

Why are you set on the destruction of humanity?

The Collective, like the Xuxaax, exist in your distant past. And like the Xuxaax, the Collective will come forward in time to inhabit the successors of mankind. Anna felt a surge of energy course through her alien body. *But you will no longer be able to experience that glorious event.* A searing pain erupted in her central mass and radiated to all of her extremities. *You have failed the Collective and must be cast out.* The pain reached Anna's head and she screamed in agony.

◆

"Anna. Anna!" Ogden shouted as Anna regained consciousness. She was screaming at the top of her lungs, and the soldier was holding her down by the shoulders. Somewhere nearby, Cletus barked defensively. "Anna, can you hear me?"

Anna's vision had been blurry and tinged with the green of the portal collapsing, but as her vision cleared, she took in her surroundings. She was laying in a hospital bed, and her wrists were bandaged. The soldier's face showed signs of prolonged worry, but bore an expression of relief. He stroked her hair before bending down to kiss her passionately on the lips. Cletus' muzzle appeared on the right side of her face and started licking it as well.

"Thank heavens!" he said as Eliezar Feldman and J. Edgar Hoover entered the room. The chair Shroud had been sitting in was lying on its back behind him. Feldman righted it and set next to the bed. Hoover glanced behind a partition before approaching Anna's bed.

"What has happened?" Anna asked. The men glanced at each.

Eventually, Ogden said, "Thanks to Cletus, we found you in the nick of time."

"The portal those monsters came through exploded," Hoover added, "and my men destroyed the creatures with righteous fury. Then the entire structure was burned to the ground. Officially, there was a gas leak, but I would like to know what was actually going on in that house."

"You have been unconscious for three days," Feldman said softly, "and the doctors could not say whether you would recover, or even regain consciousness."

Anna's eyes widened. "What happened to Conrad Fox?"

"Conrad Fox," Hoover replied, "or rather, Konrad Fuchs, was a German—" he paused to think for a moment. "I guess you would call him a German saboteur. My men have him incarcerated at a secret facility. He's telling us quite a story about German plans to conquer the world with alien assistance."

"It is true," Anna confirmed. "Fox, or whatever his name is, was sent by the Thule Society to bring the Xuxaax, those monsters, forward in time before the annihilation of their own prehistoric civilization. The German plan was to distract and weaken the American military with the invasion of those creatures."

"With the United States effectively neutralized," Feldman conjectured, "Germany could conquer Europe again."

"The Triple Entente powers are still recovering from the war," Hoover said. "They're in no condition to fend off another German offensive."

"They will be less so," Anna said, "if similar efforts by the Thule Society are not prevented in England, France, and Russia. Fox told me that there were similar plans being executed in those countries to eliminate future opposition from them."

"He never mentioned any of that to me," Maggie White's voice said meekly from beyond the partition. "I guess I was just the bait. But why did they need those other girls?"

"What other girls?" Hoover said with surprise. He moved the partition so they could see her. Maggie's wrists were also bandaged, and she kept her body tightly covered by several blankets.

"There were five other girls in that greenhouse room," White said. "They were there when I was brought there. They opened that passageway once for an instant and threw one of the girls into it. The other girls saw it and started to run away. The first girl disintegrated right before my eyes. There was a flash, and then the others all turned to stone. I guess I wasn't close enough to be affected."

"Why didn't you run away?" Feldman asked.

"I was chained to that pillar," she replied. "The other girls were locked in the greenhouse, but they weren't tied up or anything."

"The women were not turned to stone," Anna corrected. "They had been encased in it. When the first Xuxaax arrived through the portal using my psychic energy, the one that was here already and the new one preformed a dominance ritual. In the process, one of the statues was knocked over and shattered. Inside the stone fragments were pieces of a human body."

"They used your psychic energy to power the gate?" Hoover queried suspiciously.

"Yes. The being posing as Cornelius Lyton transported me back to the time of the Collective, which also predates mankind by millennia. There I was exposed to an alien book that implanted mental abilities in me that were present when I was returned to my own body. Using those powers, I established a mental connection with Ms. White, who I still thought was my sister from Teplow's dreamworld. The Collective engineered events to put me in that room to power the portal."

"Your sister from Teplow's dreamworld?!" Hoover shouted. "Brian Teplow, the mystic?"

"Dr. Rykov and her associates at the Longborough Foundation for Ethnographic Research investigated Mr. Teplow's disappearance," Feldman said. "They were able to locate him in another dimension and return him to his mother in Brooklyn."

"I find that story hard to believe," Hoover said, shaking his head, "but after what I've seen recently, I'm willing to consider the metaphysical." He turned to exit. "Rest now, ladies. I may have need of your services in the future."

As he left, a nurse came into the room. Seeing that Anna was conscious, she rushed out and returned a moment later.

"I'm sorry, gentlemen, " she said, "but Miss Rykov —"

"Doctor Rykov," Feldman said.

"— but now that Doctor Rykov is conscious, the doctor will need to conduct tests to assess her condition and determine if there are any internal injuries or other consequences from her ordeal." The nurse gestured toward the exit. "And take that dog with you."

"Yes," Feldman said, "we should let you rest. I'll check in on you tomorrow. Come on, Cletus." The dog rose and followed the librarian out of the room.

Ogden Shroud leaned over to kiss Anna on the lips again, but Anna turned her head, and he kissed her cheek instead. "I'll be back a little later," he said. Anna smiled awkwardly, and the soldier departed.

"That fella's got a thing for you," the nurse said with an unexpectedly conversational tone. "You two serious?"

"I'll say," Maggie said. "He's been here the whole time, sitting by her side with the dog." She turned to Anna with a smile. "You've got a heck of beau there."

"We only just met less than a week ago," Anna said with irritation. "He is a homeless soldier who came to my aid when I was confronted by a band of ruffians. In my gratitude, I bought him some food and got him a hotel room. He has made assumptions about our affiliation that are incorrect."

"I wouldn't jump to conclusions, dearie," the nurse said. "I'll be back with the doctor in a moment," she added, and then left the two women alone in the room.

"He's not the only one who made relationship assumptions," Maggie said with a knowing glance.

"I know now that you are not my sister from that other dimension. I confronted the alien who planted that suggestion and it confirmed that you were used to lure me to Fox's house. He did not know it, but the Xuxaax were after me the whole time."

"Well, even if we're not sisters, I think you're pretty keen, and I'd love to keep in touch. We've been through an adventure together, and that kind of thing happens for a reason."

"I would be honored to maintain our acquaintance," Anna replied.

"How about if we just be friends?" Maggie smiled broadly, and then the two of them started giggling.

Chapter 23

May 15, 1930

Anna awoke to the smell of fried eggs and bacon. Not unexpectedly, Cletus was not on the bed with her. Anna heard giggling and barking coming from outside in the yard. She rose from the bed and put on her robe and slippers before looking out the window to the backyard, where Cletus was running around the small yard being chased by three boys and two girls. The sounds of the children's laughter made Anna smile.

Anna was released from the hospital one week later. After paying her bill at the Ritz-Carlton, she went to Boston Common where she was reunited with Cletus. The big dog knocked her down and licked her face until Ogden pulled her to her feet and into his arms. When she freed herself from his embrace, Anna found that Joseph, Rosemary, Helen, and some others had gathered around them.

"Them Federals told us what happened to you," Helen said, "but Mr. Stroud said that it wasn't the whole story."

"As we understand it," Joseph interrupted, "you were successful in finding the killer, but some said that he was killed, and others said he was some kind of foreign agent who fled the country. Which is it?"

"And where are the girls?" Helen said hopefully.

Anna sighed and collected her thoughts. She looked at the faces of each of the people gathered around her. They bore expressions of hope, concern, resignation, or just curiosity. She considered how to tell them the bad news. She sighed again.

"I am afraid that your missing girls were all killed." Tears and expressions of shock erupted from Helen and some other women. The mens' faces varied between anger and acceptance. "The man the agents spoke of did represent foreign interests, and apparently he escaped from them." A disgruntled murmur rose from the assembly. "However, the killer was actually a beast that the man had acquired to collect women to use a subjects in his foul experiments."

"And my Angela was a victim of these experiments?" Helen said meekly. Anna nodded. "Did she die... No, I don't want to know." Helen's tear stained face adopted and expression of acceptance. "I knew it," she said quietly. "I knew it all along." Then she turned and walked back toward her shelter.

"So that's the end of it," Joseph said. "You achieved what you came to do and now you'll be going back home?"

"Yes," Anna said, "I will be returning to Wellersburg. But I will not forget or abandon you."

"We don't need your charity...," Joseph started to say.

"Yes, you do." Anna was direct and clear. "And I will do my part to ease your suffering." Joseph went to respond, but Anna started to walk purposefully back in the direction she had come from. "Come, Cletus." The big dog bounded after her.

"I won't abandon you either," Ogden said to the confounded crowd. "I have been reactivated and will be pursuing these foreign agents wherever they go."

◆

Exiting her bedroom, Anna closed the door behind her. She glanced down the hall to the two rear bedrooms and noted that the doors were open, and that the bunk beds in the boys' room were unmade. The girls' room was neat and tidy, but that was to be expected since they shared it with Mrs. Tidings.

Anna descended the stairs and noticed the morning mail on the sideboard. She picked up the stack of letters and flipped through them absently until she came upon a postcard. There was a drawing of Big Ben on the front, and when she turned it over, she read.

Anna,

Mr. Hoover has kept me quite busy here in London working with Special Branch to uncover the Thule Society in England. So far no luck, but there are a surprising number of unexplainable phenomena here. Maybe you can come and help us out?

I miss you,

Ogden

Anna smiled, wondering if Hoover would be upset about the secrets Lieutenant Shroud had carelessly revealed on the back of a postcard for anyone to see. Following the business in Boston, the Director of the Bureau of Investigation revealed that he had been looking into the Ogden Shroud case and other unexplainable events involving American servicemen abroad as part of an effort to expand the Bureau's jurisdiction beyond the borders of the United States.

Anna's revelation that German extremists were pursuing extra-dimensional aid to weaken the democratic powers sounded alarms in certain closed chambers of government, and, as one of only a handful of people with first-hand experience with such phenomena, Ogden Shroud was reactivated, commissioned, and assigned to a task force to pursue and deal with the threat.

He and Anna had parted ways in the same place where they had first met at South Central Station. This time, however, the soldier took her in his arms and kissed her passionately. To his surprise, Anna returned the kiss with equal enthusiasm. Anna smiled as she remembered the moment.

Suddenly, the children entered through the front door. When they saw her, the five stopped in their tracks and said, "Good morning, Miss Anna," in practiced unison. Then Cletus galloped in, walked up to Anna, and shook his wet coat, showering her with muddy water. The children laughed, and Anna found herself laughing with them.

The Hunter in the Shadows

"That's enough of that," Mrs. Tidings said, emerging from the kitchen with a towel for Anna. "Wash up and get ready for breakfast!" The children removed their galoshes, leaving them scattered across the foyer, and stormed up the stairs past Anna.

"My apologies, miss," the gray-haired woman said and ran over to close the front door. "You must be chilled to the bone! Come have some tea!"

Anna followed the nanny into the kitchen, which had been rearranged to accommodate a table large enough for six people. Woven placemats lay before each seat, bearing a plate with a fork on one side and knife and spoon on the other, all carefully arranged. In the center of the table sat a platter piled high with pancakes, another of toast, and a third of bacon. She accepted a mug of hot tea from the nanny with a smile and took a sip. Mrs. Tidings knew exactly how she liked it.

When Anna had returned from Boston, Dr. Feldman had insisted that she continue her recuperation. He hired Mrs. Tidings, an unemployed school teacher, to look after the anthropologist, now under Harold Lamb's care. The plight of the children in Boston Common had moved Anna. She had had two unused bedrooms in a largely empty house.

Through Father O'Malley, Anna had accepted five children with no one to look after them into her home. Now the once somber house was full of joy and happiness. The large living room served as playroom and classroom for her charges as well as for some other children for whom O'Malley had arranged accommodations.

Anna smiled as Jack, Wally, and Matilda entered the kitchen, followed by Sophie, who held little Homer's hand. Anna accepted the three-year-old from his older sister and sat him in her lap. Then, under the watchful eyes of their matron, the older boys pulled out the chairs for the girls, and then sat in their own chairs.

As one, the children all bowed their heads and said, "Thank you, God, for this food, for this home, and all things good. But most of all, for those we love. Amen." Then they all looked at Anna.

"Amen," Anna replied.

ABOUT THE AUTHOR

Joab Stieglitz was born and raised in Warren, New Jersey. He is an Application Consultant for a software company. He has also worked as a software trainer, a network engineer, a project manager, and a technical writer over his 30-year career. He lives in Alexandria, Virginia.

Joab is an avid tabletop RPG player and game master of horror, espionage, fantasy, and science fiction genres, including Savage Worlds (Mars, Deadlands, Agents of Oblivion, Apocalypse Prevention Inc, Herald: Tesla and Lovecraft, Thrilling Tales, and others), Call of Cthulhu, Lamentations of the Flame Princess, Pugmire, and Pathfinder.

Joab channeled his role-playing experiences in the Utgarda Series, which are pulp adventure novels with Lovecraftian influences set in the 1920's and 1930's.

You can follow Joab on Twitter @JoabStieglitz, on Facebook, and on his blog: joabstieglitz.com.

JOAB STIEGLITZ

THE OLD MAN'S REQUEST

BOOK ONE OF THE UTGARDA SERIES

The Old Man's Request
Book One of the Utgarda Series

Fifty years ago, a group of college friends dabbled in the occult and released a malign presence on the world. Now, on his deathbed, the last of the students, now a trustee of Reister University enlists the aid of three newcomers to banish the thing they summoned.

Russian anthropologist Anna Rykov, doctor Harry Lamb, and Father Sean O'Malley are all indebted the ailing trustee for their positions. Together, they pursue the knowledge and resources needed to perform the ritual.

Hampered by the old man's greedy son, the wizened director of the university library, and a private investigator with a troubled past, can they perform the ritual and banish the entity?

The Old Man's Request is a pulp adventure set in the 1920s, and the first book in the Utgarda Series.

Available in paperback and ebook formats, and as an Audible audiobook

The Missing Medium
Book Two of the Utgarda Series

While Father Sean O'Malley is summoned to Rome to discuss the "Longborough Affair" with his superiors, Russian anthropologist Anna Rykov and Doctor Harold Lamb travel to New York City where they encounter merchants, mobsters and madmen in pursuit of the spirit medium who advised their mentor shortly before the start of the whole adventure.

The Missing Medium is a pulp adventure set in the 1920s, and the second book in the Utgarda Series.

Available in paperback and ebook formats, and as an Audible audiobook

THE OTHER REALM

BOOK THREE OF
THE UTGARDA SERIES

JOAB STIEGLITZ

The Other Realm
Book Three of the Utgarda Series

Having discovered the location of Brian Teplow, Russian anthropologist Anna Rykov, doctor Harry Lamb, and Father Sean O'Malley travel to a secluded asylum to collect him. But things are not so simple, and Anna must travel to the land of Teplow's imagination to rescue him, where she finds a different world from the one suggested in the Missing Medium's journals.

The Other Realm is a pulp adventure set in the 1920s, and the third book in the Utgarda Series.

Available in paperback and ebook formats, and as an Audible audiobook

Made in the USA
Columbia, SC
30 May 2019